NOCTURNUS

NOCTURNUS

Darren Nicholls

Book Guild Publishing
Sussex, England

First published in Great Britain in 2006 by
The Book Guild Ltd
25 High Street
Lewes, East Sussex
BN7 2LU

Typesetting in Baskerville by
SetSystems Ltd, Saffron Walden, Essex

Printed in Great Britain by
CPI Bath

A catalogue record for this book is
available from the British Library

ISBN 1 84624 046 8

Acknowledgements

Firstly, I would like to thank the 'cover girls' who are, from left to right, Jessica Calderwood, Louise Calderwood, Julia Russell and Monika Krolewiak.

Secondly, I would like to thank Simon Goggin: although the jacket design is credited solely to me, Simon did have some input into the design and the jacket would not look quite as it does without his efforts.

Lastly, and most importantly, I would like to thank the film writers Eric Red and Kathryn Bigelow, who wrote the screenplay for the 1987 movie *Near Dark* (which Kathryn directed). I first saw this movie in 1991 and it impressed me so much that I wanted to write my own contemporary vampire story and so I immediately sat down and got to work.

Thirteen years later I finally succeeded!

Read and enjoy.

Chapter 1

A one-horse town; that could be considered a kind description of Fulfilment, New Mexico. The town lay some thirty
miles southwest of Tucumcari, away from the main Albu-
querque-to-Amarillo highway. Away from pretty much everywhere. Some people would have considered Fulfilment
sleepy, but the truth was it was pretty much dead.

Chloe Lamont hated Fulfilment with a passion. She was
seventeen years old and had just finished school; all she
had to look forward to now was working with her mother
up in Tucumcari—no college for her, her family couldn't
afford that. The small—no, *tiny*—town life of Fulfilment
stifled her, boxed her in, and her one and only goal was to
leave. And she would have left this hole in the world as
soon as school had finished if it hadn't been for her twin
sister Rachael. Chloe and Rachael were like chalk and
cheese, complete opposites. Chloe was exuberant and out-
going whereas Rachael was quiet and reserved. Chloe was
prone to exaggerated mood swings whereas Rachael was
nearly always unruffled. Chloe was never able to devote her
attention to one thing for any length of time before she was
onto something else; Rachael had the patience of a moun-
tain. Chloe wanted to leave Fulfilment; Rachael wanted to
stay. The sisters complemented each other perfectly.

The two girls lived in a small house with their mother,
Ruth, about a mile or so from the town's 'commercial

centre'—a grocery store, a gas station, a hardware store, a clothes shop and a few other buildings that sat either side of a dusty stretch of two-lane blacktop. The gas station had a small diner attached to it that served the usual short-order fare found all over the USA and was also equipped with a root beer and soda fountain. This place served as the gathering point for Fulfilment's small cadre of unfulfilled underagers. The unfulfilled overagers had the luxury of sitting in the town's only bar—the Rancher's Retreat, a dive that served tepid beer and had a dilapidated pool table and a jukebox that had not had new records put in it since the mid-eighties. Fulfilment was no place going nowhere fast.

Chloe had had yet another blazing row with her mother, a common occurrence these days and it hurt her that things were like this. She loved her momma, loved her dearly, but Ruth Lamont could be a real pain, especially to a seventeen-year-old with dreams that were far, far bigger than this town. She had stormed out of the house, taking only enough time to grab her favourite brown leather jacket, and as always found herself being drawn to the only place there was to be drawn to, the small diner at the centre of town. At night the commercial centre was an oasis of light in an otherwise pitch darkness and despite her foul mood Chloe couldn't help but be lifted as she neared the now-closed stores that were bathed in harsh, white light. As she entered the lighted area her eyes roamed left and right hoping, futilely she knew, that she would see something new, something different.

That night she did.

Walking slowly down the street on the other side was a woman, a *stranger*! She looked to be in her mid-thirties and was dressed in dusty, faded, pale denim jeans, a dusty, faded, pale denim jacket and dusty, faded, brown leather cowboy boots. Despite her road-worn appearance the

2

woman, to Chloe's eyes at least, seemed to positively *shine*. She wasn't devastatingly pretty but she certainly was attractive, age lending maturity to her looks, and her dark hair was shoulder length and luxuriously thick. Her skin was very pale, almost white, and this only highlighted her ruby lips and dark eyes. Chloe was struck statue-still by an incredible, indescribable beauty in the woman and she just stared at her. The woman was looking all around her and taking in the sights, not that here was much to see here. After about ten seconds she became aware of Chloe's regard and stopped walking and looked directly at the teenager. Chloe had to swallow hard as her eyes met the woman's; there was an unending depth to that gaze and Chloe found herself almost drowning in it. Then the woman broke the spell by giving Chloe a warm, genuine smile. Chloe smiled back and the woman began to walk towards her with a steady, even gait that made it appear that she was gliding over the ground rather than walking on it.

As she approached, she said, 'Hi!'

'Hi there!' replied Chloe. 'I haven't seen you round here before.'

'That's because I'm only passing through,' replied the woman. Her voice had that wonderful, lilting brogue that could only come from Ireland.

'I guessed that,' said Chloe with genuine regret, and her face mirrored the disappointment in her voice.

'Hey!' said the woman. 'What's wrong?'

'This place,' replied Chloe with a deep sigh. 'It's so dull around here that even a brief encounter with a stranger is a high point.'

'It can't be that bad?' responded the woman.

'You don't live here,' replied Chloe with a wry grin. 'And be thankful for that.'

'You look like you could use some company for a while,' suggested the woman.

'I sure could!' Chloe answered with a hopeful smile. 'If you can stand it here for more than ten minutes, that is.'

The woman laughed, a delighted sound, then she stuck out her hand and introduced herself. 'I'm Maggie O'Hearn.'

'Chloe Lamont,' replied the teenager, shaking the proffered hand. The woman smiled warmly again and Chloe felt her stomach turn watery and her legs weaken. Although she would never admit it to anyone, Chloe was already absolutely infatuated with Maggie. She gave the woman a really shy smile and as Maggie's smile warmed even more, Chloe's heart started to flutter.

'It's good to meet you, Chloe. Is there any place to go round here?' That burr in Maggie's voice caused Chloe's heart to melt.

The two of them went to the only place there was to go to, the small diner. There they bought a couple of root beers and sat at a table in the far corner. There were only a handful of people in the diner that night, a group of teenagers; they were sitting at one table talking idly and without any real animation.

'Is it always like this?' Maggie asked, gesturing over her shoulder with her thumb towards the teenagers.

Chloe looked to where Maggie was pointing and replied, 'This is a pretty good night, they're usually more lifeless than this.'

Maggie rolled her eyes and Chloe continued, 'That's what I mean about this town, there's nothing here really. I'm surprised it hasn't died yet.'

'There's a lot of places like this in America,' said Maggie in a quiet voice. 'I've been to a few of them and they're all the same. Dull and directionless.'

Hearing Maggie's accent made Chloe wonder what she was doing all the way out in the middle of nowhere. She knew that there was a concentration of people of Irish descent in the northeastern states but none of them ever reached here.

'So where're you from?' Chloe asked.

'Originally I'm from Boston, Massachusetts although that was ... some time ago.' The way Maggie said this made Chloe look up. When she said 'some time ago' she made it sound like it had been many decades rather than years. Chloe looked at her new friend a little more closely and saw that although Maggie looked to be in her mid-thirties there was a quality to her that made an accurate guess of her age impossible.

'Where do you live now?' Chloe asked.

'Everywhere,' replied Maggie with a shrug of her shoulders and a widening of her arms. 'I spend most of my time travelling around the country.'

'What do you do?'

'Travel,' replied Maggie with an impish grin. 'I don't do much of anything, I'm what you'd call bone idle, but that suits me just fine.'

Chloe snorted at this and said, 'You're bone idle and I'm bone weary.'

'Aw, come on!' Maggie exclaimed quietly. 'It can't be that bad. You're what, sixteen?'

'Seventeen actually.'

'Seventeen! Your life has hardly started and you're talking like it's already over.'

'That's what this town does to you,' said Chloe with deep seriousness. 'The unending monotony saps your spirit, erodes your will.'

Maggie gave Chloe an assessing look before asking, 'So what do you wish for?'

'In all honesty,' replied Chloe after a couple of moments of thought, 'something more interesting, more varied than here. Hell! Something different at the very least. Those guys over there,' she pointed to the teenagers, 'they're only hanging together cause there's no one else to hang with. There's hardly anything here so your options are really limited.'

'You don't hang with them?' asked Maggie, indicating the other group.

'Used to,' replied Chloe. 'But I just don't feel right with them, you know?'

Maggie nodded understanding. The conversation petered to a halt then and during the silence Maggie directed a penetrating gaze at Chloe, measuring, assessing. Chloe was just starting to become uncomfortable with this when Maggie suddenly said, 'Come with me.' She finished the rest of her root beer. 'I want to show you something.'

'What?' asked Chloe, her curiosity piqued.

'You'll see,' replied Maggie, and her expression turned mysterious.

Chloe was normally a sensible girl and wouldn't just walk off with an almost total stranger, but there was something about Maggie that said she was trustworthy. Chloe shrugged her shoulders and finished the rest of her drink—why the hell not? There wasn't anything else to do around here.

Maggie led Chloe up the road and away from the pool of light that was the gas station, away from her home. They passed the Rancher's Retreat—there were a couple of vehicles in the parking lot and Chloe recognised the two pickup trucks and the station wagon, although the Winnebago was new to her. As they were passing the bar the sound of Starship's 'We Built This City' came from within.

'I wish they'd get some new records for that fuckin' jukebox!' Chloe muttered to herself sourly.

'It is a bit old,' agreed Maggie. 'But still a good tune.'

'Not when you've heard it as many times as I have,' Chloe shot back. She was a little startled—she had muttered that comment to herself and Maggie had heard her from several yards away. This woman must have excellent hearing if she caught Chloe's almost-silent comment. Another thing that struck her about Maggie was her sure, confident step along the road in the pitch dark, and so she asked, 'Can you see where you're going?'

'Of course I can!' replied Maggie over her shoulder. 'The question is, can you?'

'I've lived out here all my life,' said Chloe. 'Night sight is something you develop.'

'I know exactly what you mean,' Maggie said. It was a sentence that was loaded with other, hidden meanings.

After an indeterminate length of time Maggie suddenly stopped. She then spread her arms wide, stood on tiptoes and breathed deeply. When she exhaled it was a sound of pure contentment. Chloe turned around and was surprised to see how far she had come. The pool of light that marked where the centre of town stood was a tiny blob of white, miles away it seemed. Chloe almost screamed when she felt her head grabbed in two strong hands, and then a gentle voice whispered in her ear, 'Don't look at that, it'll only blind you. I brought you out here so that you can truly see!'

Chloe felt the hands turn her head back toward the pitch blackness and away from the light.

'Look out there,' said Maggie in an intense whisper. 'What do you see, what do you hear?'

Chloe couldn't help giggling at this question; it seemed a little silly. 'I see only darkness,' she replied. 'I hear nothing, silence.'

Maggie's voice took on warmer tones when she said, 'Then look and listen harder but don't just use your eyes and ears.'

Chloe giggled again—this was silly! But kinda fun too. She did as Maggie said, opened her eyes and ears wide to the night and . . .

'Ohh!' she cried quietly and brought a hand to her throat. Briefly, very briefly she had sensed something, something that seemed totally overwhelming.

'You just touched upon it,' said Maggie knowingly. 'The full force of the night. If you open yourself up to it fully the darkness will blind you, the silence will deafen.'

'It felt enormous,' said Chloe in a querulous voice. 'But comforting too.'

'The night is,' said Maggie dreamily.

Chloe closed her eyes this time, calmed herself and then reached out once more. Forewarned about what to expect, she danced around the edges of the night's immense size and delighted in the sensations it gave her. She gently twirled with her arms spread wide and her head tilted backwards, her eyes regarding the cosmos above her.

'The stars are so bright!' she marvelled.

'That they are,' agreed Maggie, also looking to the heavens.

Chloe had no idea how long she had stood out in the middle of nowhere, delighting in the night, but she suddenly became aware of Maggie standing very close to her.

'Do you really hate it here?' Maggie asked.

'You've no idea,' replied Chloe in a voice that conveyed so much despair and disillusionment. 'There are no prospects in a place like this. My family doesn't have much money so there's no chance of college. I've just finished school and all I've got to look forward to now is working in a shitty factory with my mom up in Tucumcari.' She turned her head and found Maggie's face almost pressed against hers; they were eye to eye and Chloe once again felt the drowning sensation as she sunk into the bottomless depths of Maggie's gaze.

'I can take you away from here, Chloe,' Maggie said with all seriousness. 'But you'll have to give up everything that

8

has gone before. Once you set foot upon the path I walk, there's no turning back.'

'And just what is your path?' asked Chloe.

'I'm one with the night.'

'And what exactly does that mean?' Chloe was puzzled.

'Let's just say that I live a lifestyle that's radically different to yours,' Maggie answered. 'It has its drawbacks but they're *far* outweighed by the benefits. If I were to tell you you'd just dismiss me as crazy—you have to experience it to fully appreciate it.'

'But once I set foot down that road there's no coming back,' Chloe finished.

'Exactly!' said Maggie. 'It's an all-or-nothing gamble.'

'No half way?' Chloe ventured.

Maggie blew a raspberry. 'It's going half way with things that stifles you, stunts you. To truly grow you have to truly *live.*'

Chloe folded her arms across her chest and demanded, 'You're not some talent scout for a porno filmmaker are you?'

Maggie's derisory laugh answered that one.

'Guess not,' Chloe murmured to herself. 'Drug dealer?'

'The sensations of the night are the only drug I need.' And the earnest way in which Maggie said this convinced Chloe that Maggie was telling nothing but the truth on that one.

'What are you then?' she asked the woman.

'I'm one with the night,' Maggie repeated. She then pulled Chloe into a gentle embrace and whispered in her ear, 'Do you want to be one with the night? To share its delights with me for all eternity?'

'Shit!' said Chloe, laughing. 'I've got nothing to look forward to here, so yeah! Why the hell not?' She obviously hadn't heard Maggie's last words.

Maggie didn't say any more after that and instead began to gently nuzzle and kiss Chloe's face and neck. Chloe was a little alarmed by this at first but her alarm quickly vanished when she realised how good it felt. She half closed her eyes and began to whimper with sheer pleasure. Maggie kept kissing and nuzzling and Chloe began to loosen all her ties and go with the joyful flow Maggie was creating.

'OW!' cried Chloe as she was jerked out of the slipstream of pleasure by a stinging pain in her neck. She put a hand to the area of pain and it felt wet. All thoughts of the night, of pleasure had evaporated and Chloe was centring on one simple fact. 'You bit me!'

'Just a gentle nip,' replied Maggie in a heavy, laden voice. 'Come with me.' And she held out her hand.

'I'm not going anywhere with you!' shouted Chloe. 'You bit me, you fuckin' weirdo!'

'Chloe, please,' Maggie said gently and she took a step forward. 'You'll need me with you when you change. And afterwards too.' She stretched her arm towards Chloe again.

But Chloe wasn't listening. 'Get the fuck away from me!' she yelled, slapping Maggie's outstretched hand away and backing up quickly.

'Chloe!' Maggie took another step towards the teenager, her posture and voice now containing some urgency.

'Fuck off!' screamed Chloe and with that she turned and ran. Ran towards the small blob of white light that marked the centre of town, on the other side of which lay her home.

When she had gone off into the darkness with Maggie she had marvelled at just how far the two of them had walked. Now she was cursing that distance—she was quite a way from her house. She could cut across country and bypass town, that would save some time, but that was risky. Even with good night vision like she had she could still put her foot down a hole and twist her ankle. Or break her leg.

She was normally a good runner but after only a short

distance her feet began to feel leaden, her legs weak and wobbly and all she could do was stagger down the road in a lurching, stumbling gait. She continually looked over her shoulder, both praying for a car to come along and give her a lift and fearing Maggie right on her heels. As she neared town she saw that the quality of the night had changed quite dramatically—she was beginning to see some distant objects. It was nearly sunrise.

Christ! How long had she been out there?

Momma was gonna throw a real shitfit over this one and that was for sure! One benefit of the approaching dawn was that she could see where she was going much better and so left the road and cut across the dusty, rocky countryside.

As it got lighter Chloe got slower and slower until she was only stumbling along at a normal walking pace. Also she was beginning to feel sick, really sick, like she was coming down with something. She was feeling hot and as it got lighter she felt hotter and she got weaker. She was losing her balance and falling to the floor quite frequently now, her eyes swam in and out of focus and when she exhaled she gave off a faint moan. She shambled along in a fog of fever heat and disorientation, but when she finally looked up to get her bearings she was greeted with a sight that sent her spirits soaring.

Less than a mile away was her home.

Ruth Lamont was both seething and sorrowful. Angry at the recent behaviour of her daughter Chloe but also deeply sad about the reason for Chloe's outbursts: the dull life Ruth had given her daughters by raising them in Fulfilment. Ruth felt unfulfilled here, so heaven knew how a seventeen-year-old would feel. This most recent argument had been for the same reason as most of the others: there was nothing here for Chloe. Ruth was surprised that Chloe hadn't upped and left already, but as she sat at the kitchen table watching the dawn creep into the sky she knew the reason why. Sitting opposite her, keeping vigil with her, was Chloe's twin, Rachael. Rachael was the reason Chloe was still here and as long as she stayed so would Chloe, becoming more and more disconsolate with each passing day.

Why didn't they go off together? Simply because Rachael loved the quiet pulse of life here and had no desire to leave. She loved the simple, familiar routine and the vast expanse of New Mexican desert that was the backdrop to their home. Rachael didn't have any starry-eyed dreams of going to a big city or becoming someone famous. She took what she had and made the most of that without wishing for more.

For the hundredth time during the small hours Ruth bit back the urge to burst into tears. She hadn't meant to become bogged down here—in many ways she had been like Chloe was now, full of wanderlust and curiosity. In fact, she had only been passing through Fulfilment on her way to California when something both wondrous and disastrous had happened.

She had fallen in love.

Jackson Lamont had been a miner, back in the days when there were mines around here, and when Ruth had first laid eyes on him she had fallen head over heels for him. To give Jackson credit, he had instantly fallen for her too. Within six months they were married and six months after that she had given birth to Chloe and Rachael and life for Ruth couldn't have been sweeter. Then disaster had struck when the girls were just four years old. The shaft Jackson and eight other miners had been working in collapsed, killing them all and Ruth's dreams of happy ever after. Ruth's life had then become nothing but duty to raise her two daughters on her own and she had done a damn fine job of it too. Despite the now-constant rows, Chloe had grown up into a bright, intelligent and kind young woman,

12

Rachael had too. Ruth had always meant to leave Fulfilment and give her daughters somewhere with more variety to grow up in. But it hadn't happened, there was never enough money for a venture like that and as the years rolled by Ruth became more and more embedded here. She sighed bitterly at the way things were at the moment, wishing she could do something to make things better for Chloe, for all of them.

She was brought out of her reverie when Rachael suddenly stood up from her seat; she was gazing intently out of the kitchen window. Ruth followed her daughter's gaze and saw what Rachael saw.

A distant figure stumbling across the desert towards the house.

Rachael quickly went outside through the kitchen door and stood on the back porch, straining her eyes to get a clearer view of the approaching figure. Ruth was right behind her daughter and they both identified the person simultaneously.

It was Chloe.

But something was very wrong; she was staggering towards them and falling to her knees every couple of steps, kicking up quite a bit of dust. But the dust wasn't just rising up from the floor; it was coming off Chloe too.

And to Rachael it looked more like smoke.

Mother and daughter regarded each other with mounting alarm, and as one began to run towards Chloe.

Chloe had never felt so awful before in all her life. The sun had now cleared the horizon to her right and as its rays fell upon her she began to burn, really burn. The heat was unbearable and despite her dulled senses she was nevertheless alarmed to see smoke pouring out of her jacket and jeans although it looked a bit like steam. However, there was smoke also pouring out of her reddening skin and that really freaked her. And that smell!

That's me, she thought miserably. *That's the smell of me burnin' up.*

She raised her head to the house again and saw two figures running towards her, screaming her name.

'Raych, Momma!' Chloe tried to cry out their names but all she could manage was a hoarse whisper. Then another smell assaulted her nostrils, singeing hair. She knew then that she was in *serious* trouble and redoubled her efforts to reach her family.

Rachael and Ruth had set off at a dead run towards Chloe but as soon as they had done so a Winnebago had appeared from behind a ridge to the south-east and was speeding along one of the many tracks that criss-crossed the desert.

And it was heading straight for Chloe.

Rachael instinctively knew that this vehicle meant to take her sister away and she screamed Chloe's name. Despite already running flat out she was able to find new reserves and sprinted towards her sister, leaving her mother in her wake. But Rachael knew in her heart of hearts that the bus would reach Chloe first.

Chloe heard her name screamed, saw her sister sprint towards her, but she felt that something was bearing down upon her. She turned to see a Winnebago speeding towards her; as it neared the driver jammed its brakes on and the side door flapped open. As the bus passed her at a speed approaching a fast walking pace, two figures reached out and grabbed Chloe. She saw that one was wearing a long trench coat and the other was in denims. Both figures' heads were fully swathed by towels save the eyes, which were covered with tinted pilot's goggles complete with nose guards; their hands were inside leather gloves. Chloe was surprised and not a little frightened when they bodily lifted her up and hauled her into the bus. As the side door slammed shut, the one in the trench coat turned to the driver and said, 'Got her!'

'And we're outta here!' came the reply from the front.

Chloe felt the bus lurch as the driver hauled on the steering wheel and turned the vehicle through one hundred and eighty degrees; then she felt a surge as the gas pedal was stamped on.

The interior of the Winnebago was very dark—all the windows had been covered—and Chloe was extremely grateful for this. Out of the sun, the burning sensation she had been feeling had stopped although she could still feel the residual pain. Her initial relief was quickly ended when she realised that she had been snatched from off her very own doorstep by strangers. Strangers who had covered their faces; she began to thrash and moan.

'Let me go! Let me go!'

She felt her shoulders grabbed by strong hands, and a familiar voice full of the Emerald Isle sounded from one of the figures. 'Easy! Easy! You're safe now!'

'Please! I want to go home! I want my momma!' cried Chloe.

'Easy now, Chloe,' said the familiar voice in soothing tones.

'I want my mommy!' Chloe sobbed.

Then the speaker pulled off the towel and goggles and Chloe saw that it was Maggie O'Hearn.

'You're out of the sun,' she said to the distraught girl. 'You're safe now.'

'Please!' Chloe begged. She grabbed Maggie's jacket and started crying. 'Let me go home!'

'Chloe,' said Maggie in a soft, lulling tone, pulling the girl into her arms. 'It's daytime. You should sleep now. Go to sleep, Chloe. Go to sleep.'

Sleep. Yes, that sounded right to Chloe's confused brain.

Sleep was exactly the right thing. She stared into Maggie's depthless eyes and felt a gentle hand stroke her forehead. Maggie crooned over and over, 'Sleep now, Chloe, go to sleep.'

'Sleep,' Chloe's voice slurred and her head lolled as slumber began to wash over her like an advancing tide. She descended into darkness.

Chapter 2

Sheriff Earl Bergman was out of his depth and he knew it. Policing Fulfilment was a relatively easy job as crime was nearly non-existent here, one of the benefits of everybody knowing everybody else. The few crimes that did take place within his jurisdiction were invariably perpetrated by people passing through and a quick call to his long-time friend Jim Wagner—Captain James Wagner of the New Mexico state patrol—gave Earl the necessary aid in bringing those felons to justice.

However, this was different. In his twenty-three years as an officer of the law Earl had never had to deal with an abduction of a Fulfilment resident before. This on top of another first that had come to him that same morning—FBI Special Agent Samantha Morrell.

He was out at Ruth Lamont's place and Agent Morrell had come with him. She had tried to detain him with her business but when she heard about the abduction she said she would accompany him. She wanted to make sure that this incident wasn't related to her case.

'Goddamn it, Earl!' Ruth was a mixture of emotions, anger and worry, fear and aggression. 'My daughter was snatched from this very spot over four hours ago and you only come by now?'

Earl was at a loss; normally standard procedure would kick in and Earl was great at standard procedure. However, this situation was not standard and he didn't know what to do next. He tried to placate Ruth but that just made her angrier, he tried to take control of the situation but Ruth, a woman he had known for over seventeen years, just kept railing at him. He was getting nowhere and it was then that Agent Morrell stepped in and took over. Earl Bergman felt a surge of gratitude to her for that.

'Mrs. Lamont.' began the Fed. 'I am Special Agent Morrell from the FBI.' She showed Ruth her ID. 'I'm here investigating a case and I need to make sure that this incident isn't connected with my investigation. Could you please tell me exactly what happened here?'

Ruth tried a couple of times to speak but all she could manage was tears; it was Rachael who gave Sam the story.

'Chloe's a restless girl,' began Rachael. 'This town is far too small for her and that's resulted in a lot of rows recently.'

Morrell saw Ruth nodding sad agreement through her tears.

'There was another argument last night and as usual Chloe stormed out of the house. There's only one place to go round here at night, and that's the diner.'

'Diner?' queried Sam.

'Yeah,' said Rachael, looking slightly embarrassed. 'It's what passes for one round here, it's attached to the gas station and it does burgers and sodas and not much else. Anyway, after Chloe stormed out we didn't bother followin' her as we knew where she was goin' and she normally comes home around midnight at the latest. But last night she didn't come home and me and Momma stayed up all night waitin' for her. Then around dawn we saw a person comin' across here towards the house. We were in the kitchen at the time and we went out onto the porch to see who it was. As the person got closer we could see that it was Chloe and she looked like she was in trouble.'

18

'How so?' asked Morrell.

'She was staggerin' along and fallin' down every couple of feet. Anyway, as soon as we saw it was Chloe we ran out toward her and that's when the Winnebago appeared.'

'What direction did it come from?' the agent asked.

Rachael pointed in a southeasterly direction. 'It came from behind that ridge over there. This part of the desert's riddled with all sorts of tracks that you can drive vehicles along, even a big one like that bus.'

Morrell saw Sheriff Bergman nod affirmation of this.

'I saw that it was headin' for Chloe,' continued Rachael. 'I just knew that it was after her so I ran as hard as I could but it got to her before I did. Someone, or maybe two people, I couldn't see clearly, reached out of the side door and pulled Chloe in. Then the bus turned right around and went back the way it came.'

Samantha digested this information but she could see that Rachael was holding something back.

'What aren't you telling me, Rachael?' she asked the girl gently.

Rachael looked uncomfortable, stared at the floor and mumbled, 'You'd just think I was imaginin' things.'

'Please tell me,' said Morrell gently.

Rachael paused, collecting her thoughts so she could describe what she had seen properly. 'Chloe was stumblin' along and fallin' over every few feet and so was kickin' up quite a bit of dust but . . .' She hesitated and Sam gave her an encouraging look. 'When she got up I could see that stuff was risin' up off of her too and it didn't look like dust.'

'What did it look like, Rachael?' asked Sam, her attention now firmly fixed on the girl.

Rachael turned stricken eyes first to her mother and then to the agent. 'It looked like smoke risin' up off her, it looked like she was about to burst into flames.'

Earl Bergman turned his attention to Morrell on hearing

19

this and was more than a little scared when he saw the deathly pale look on the agent's face.

'Jesus!' Sam breathed quietly to herself. 'I came within four hours of them?' She pondered a moment and then asked, 'What can you remember about the Winnebago, Rachael?'

'Not much,' answered Rachael honestly. 'My attention was on my sister.'

'But you saw it so you'll remember things about it. What did it look like?'

Rachael thought a moment and then said, 'It was old, beat up, looked like it had done lots of miles. There were dents all over the body and the engine didn't sound too hot either. I couldn't tell you what the licence plate was, though.'

'That's okay, the bus was most likely stolen for sure. What about the windshield, what did that look like?' Sam asked with quiet intensity.

Rachael looked puzzled by the question but she thought for a few moments and then gave Morrell an incredulous look. She paused to collect herself again and then said, 'The sun was just above the horizon.' She pointed off to the east. 'And the bus was comin' straight down this track so the sun was shinin' on the sides and not on the windshield. I know this sounds crazy, but thinkin' about it I would swear that the windshield was covered with tinfoil.'

'With a dark strip running through the middle of it from side to side?' offered Morrell, using her hands to panto-mime the strip.

'Yeah!' said Rachael. 'That's exactly how it was.'

Morrell turned to Bergman then and said, 'Sheriff, this incident *is* connected with the case I'm investigating and therefore comes under federal jurisdiction now.'

'You're sure?' asked Bergman. He was puzzled by this, extremely puzzled.

'Almost positive,' replied Morrell. 'The occupants of that vehicle are on the Bureau's wanted list.'

'In that case,' began Earl, 'any assistance that my office can offer is yours, although it isn't much I'm afraid. Fulfilment just isn't a hotbed of crime.'

'As long as you don't mind my taking over an investigation that's on your turf.'

Earl held up a placating hand and said, 'The FBI has far more resources for resolving this matter than my small office—I have absolutely no resentment whatsoever.' The plain truth was he was relieved that someone else was taking this over from him.

'Thank you,' said Sam. She then turned to mother and daughter and asked, 'Do you have a photo of Chloe that I could have? It'll make tracking her a little easier.'

'Sure,' said Rachael, fishing into her back pocket and pulling out what looked very much like a man's leather wallet. She opened it up and riffled through the contents before pulling out a rather dog-eared but nevertheless good-quality photo of Chloe Lamont.

Sam looked first at the photo and then at Rachael. At first glance the two girls looked identical but if you studied them a bit closer you could make out differences—they were small but they were there.

'Thank you very much for this,' said Sam, waving the photo. 'I'll try and keep you posted either personally or through Sheriff Bergman if I have any new news and an opportunity to pass it on. Now, if you'll excuse me I want to get under way while the trail is still warm.'

'I just want my daughter back!' said Ruth. She had stopped crying now but her eyes glistened with more unshed tears.

Samantha Morrell nodded but did not have the heart to tell her that there was probably no way back for Chloe, not now.

21

She had gone too far.

Sam and Earl bade the Lamonts goodbye and headed to their cars. Before Sam got into her car she said, 'Just a couple more things, Sheriff Bergman. Firstly, I need to speak to the person manning the diner last night and see if they saw anything.'

'That'll be Jack Astle,' said Bergman. 'He runs the gas station too, so he'll be up already.'

'Also, does this town have a bar?'

'Sure does,' replied Bergman. 'The Rancher's Retreat, it's just up the road a little. Mike Parney runs the place and he lives in a trailer at the back.'

'Thank you, Sheriff. Now, if you'll excuse me I'll bid you good day and thank you for your assistance here.'

'Not a problem, Agent Morrell, I hope you catch them and soon.'

'I'll do my utmost on that last.' And with that Sam shook hands with Bergman, then climbed into her car and headed into town. Her first stop was the gas station.

'Oh yeah, Chloe was in here last night,' said Astle. 'In here with some stranger.'

'You're sure it was a stranger?' asked Morrell.

'Oh yeah,' said Astle, nodding hugely. 'Everyone knows everyone round here, so strangers get noticed.'

'Was it this woman by any chance?' asked Morrell, producing an e-fit photograph of Maggie O'Hearn and showing him.

Astle looked at it for a second and replied, 'Yup, that's who Chloe was with last night.'

'You're sure?' Sam asked. She noticed that he had only glanced at the photo; she wanted him to be absolutely positive.

'Oh yeah,' replied Astle, nodding vigorously again. 'The woman was dressed all in light blue denim, quite dusty and worn. She was really strikin' too, you know, beautiful as opposed to just pretty.'

Sam nodded; she knew exactly what he meant, although 'alluring' would be a more accurate description of Maggie.

'Did they leave here together?' she asked him.

'Yeah, must've been round nine-thirty or maybe closer to ten when they left. They was real chatty too, like they'd known one another years.'

Morrell looked thoughtful a moment and then asked, 'Is there anywhere around here where someone could park a Winnebago out of sight and it not be noticed?'

'Not round here, no,' answered Astle, shaking his head. 'It's pretty much all that you see is all that there is. You wanna hide somethin' like a Winnebago then Tucumcari is your nearest place, that's only thirty miles away and it's a lot bigger 'n here.'

'Thank you for your time, Mr. Astle, have a good day.'

'You too, Ma'am.'

After leaving the gas station Sam travelled up the road to the Rancher's Retreat and knocked on the door of the trailer. Mike Parney was up but looked like he'd only just got up. His face brightened when he saw Sam at his door.

His smile faded a little when Sam showed him her ID and asked 'Mike Parney?' He nodded. 'I'm special agent Morrell from the FBI. I need to ask you a couple of questions. Do you have time?'

'Sure thing, Agent Morrell, how can I help you?' Parney replied.

'Did any strangers come into your bar last night?'

'Yeah,' Mike said. 'Three women, never seen them before.'

'Was it these women?' asked Morrell, producing the e-fit again along with two drawings.

Parney studied them for a few moments and then replied,

'Yeah, those three were in last night, that one...' He indicated Maggie O'Hearn. 'She left after a little while but the other two stayed until closin' time. No one bothered them though, it looked pretty obvious that they were dykes.'

'I don't suppose you saw what vehicle they were in?' Sam asked.

'I didn't,' replied Parney. 'But Loy Hogan mentioned there was a Winnebago in the lot. Don't get many of them round here.'

'Thank you very much for your time, Mister Parney,' said Sam. 'I'll bid you good day.'

'Not a problem, Agent Morrell.'

Back in the car, Sam got out a local area map and studied it.

'After snatching Chloe you'd need to get to somewhere safe and quickly,' she murmured to herself.

The map showed her that there were a fair number of settlements within an hour's drive of Fulfilment and all of them looked to be quite a bit bigger, so any of them could have been the group's destination. Furthermore, Chloe was snatched at just after five this morning, which meant that the group would have gone to ground by six at the latest. Morrell knew that the chances of anyone having seen the Winnebago pull up in their town at that time would be small indeed.

'Where did you go?' she asked of the air, her eyes distant.

She had been following them for a long time now and knew that just dashing off in any direction was the easiest way to lose them. These girls were hard to track and in order to maintain pursuit you had to keep a certain distance. Fall too far back, though, and they'd disappear altogether. Sam bit back a few curses and looked at the map again but knew that it wouldn't tell her where they'd gone. Her gaze then fell on the photo of Chloe Lamont and she regarded it with an intense stare.

24

'You, my dear, could be just the break I'm looking for.'

She then reached into an inside pocket and got her cellphone out. She dialled a number.

'New Mexico state patrol,' answered the voice on the other end.

'May I speak with Captain James Wagner, please?' enquired Sam.

'Who's calling?'

'Special Agent Samantha Morrell from the FBI.'

'One moment please, I'll see if he's available.' The phone line went silent as Sam was put on hold. A few seconds later . . .

'Hey Sam! How's things?' Wagner's voice was cheery.

'Not too bad Jim, not too bad,' answered Sam, equally cheery and with a smile on her face. Sam had had several dealings with Wagner in the past on other cases and the two of them got along extremely well. 'Listen, I'm in the town of Fulfilment at the moment.'

'What the hell are you doin' in that pissy little burg?' Wagner exclaimed.

'Just passing through,' replied Sam. 'And a good job too, because four hours previously the group I'm after were here. They snatched a seventeen-year-old girl as well.'

'Christ! That's a lucky break! For you I mean, not the girl.'

'You don't have to tell me!' Sam shot back good-humouredly. 'I need to get to Albuquerque in a hurry, so can you tell your boys on the road that I'm about and speeding?'

'Sure thing, Sam,' replied Wagner, his voice serious. 'If you get the chance keep me posted on further developments.'

'I'll try, Jim,' Sam half-promised. 'But I get the feeling I'm gonna be doing a lot of driving in the next few days. This group I'm after just doesn't know how to stay put.'

'Give me the details of your car and I'll let my boys know you're about so you don't get held up.'

Sam gave Wagner the make, model and licence plate of her car and then hit the road. She kept a steady eighty-five all the way to the state capital.

Ten years. That's how long Samantha Morrell had been on this case. Ten long, lonely, frustrating years. She was forty-two years old, unmarried and childless but still able to have those things should she really want them. She was still an attractive woman with a pleasing figure, strong facial features and long, blonde hair; she could definitely draw men's eyes. She had joined the FBI at the age of twenty-six after five successful years as a homicide detective with the Atlanta PD. Atlanta, now there was a place to be a police officer! Her five years as a detective had been preceded by three years as a patrolwoman on the streets of that city, so she had had some solid grounding before joining the FBI. Once she had become an agent she had turned into something of a rising star in the Bureau. Every case she was assigned to she had brought to a conclusion—although not necessarily a conviction, as the 'justice' system in America depended on how much money you had to spend on your lawyer. She attained the rank of special agent after masterminding an operation that not only completely smashed a prolific people-smuggling ring but also brought down the high-flying accountancy firm that laundered the profits for them.

Then ten years ago Samantha was assigned to a new case—two multiple murders, one in Ohio and the other in Indiana. The murders were over two hundred miles apart, in two different states, and it was only because the two state police chiefs were friends that any connection was made; otherwise the FBI would never have been brought in. The way in which the victims had been killed—their throats had been torn out—pointed to one small group being responsible.

Morrell went about this case in her usual diligent fashion and was actually able to discover two more multiple murders in the northeast that were very similar to the killings she was investigating. In a seven-month period this group had killed a total of eighteen people. Sam went to the Behavioural Sciences Unit for help but they could only tell her that the perps were not serial killers, just random ones.

With very little in the way of clues to go on, Sam spent a hellish time trying to follow their trail. Every month or three there would be another multiple killing in Kentucky or Virginia or Pennsylvania or some other state. The killings wouldn't be discovered for a week or so, which meant that Sam was just floundering in this group's wake. However, she persevered and was able to set up a makeshift communications network across the northern states, which finally brought forth some more clues. Every once in a while a witness could be found who claimed to have seen strangers in the area around the time the killings took place. Sam decided to get artist's impressions of these strangers and found that in five of the killings the same four people had been seen.

One killing is chance, two are coincidence, but five?

Sam was of the opinion that these four people could very well be the killers. That was an eye-opener too, as they turned out to be women. A redhead, a brunette and two with blonde hair; all were described as attractive looking, aged thirty something and they were only ever seen at night. One was dressed in denims and one in black leather; another wore a long coat and men's pants and shirt. The last wore a brown leather jacket and dark blue jeans.

So far, they had a tally of thirty-eight victims to their name.

That was about all the information that she could glean about them and she was still nowhere near catching up with them, let alone catching them. Then, two years into the case, she was finally able to confront them, and what a nightmare that incident had turned into.

After following in their wake for so long, Sam finally got a lead which enabled her to catch right up with them. They had killed another group of people in Wenatchee, Washington state and had stolen their vehicle. Members of the Tacoma PD had discovered the vehicle parked at the rear of a truck stop late one afternoon and had decided to call in the FBI rather than move in and try and apprehend the killers themselves. Sam was in the FBI's Seattle office at the time and arrived in Tacoma with five other agents within an hour of the van being discovered. There they joined forces with Washington state troopers and Tacoma police officers and overall control of the operation was given to Sam. As these women had killed numerous people over nearly three years no one was taking any chances. All the state troopers were armed with assault rifles and the Tacoma officers had high-powered handguns, and the SWAT team was there also. A total of thirty-eight law enforcers moved in on the vehicle just after sundown. Just as the four women emerged from it.

They were caught right out in the open, surrounded on three sides by enough firepower to give an infantry unit pause and yet they didn't surrender. The firefight that ensued reminded Morrell of a Hollywood western with all guns a-blazing. The sound of gunfire was absolutely deafening, but for all that firepower the result was not what was expected. At the end of the gunfight twenty-one law enforcers were dead, four of them from the FBI. The seventeen survivors all had various injuries; Sam suffered a severe concussion when the fuel tank of a nearby car exploded and sent her flying. What frightened Morrell and the survivors the most was that despite being gunned down numerous times the four women kept getting up again and shooting back. When they ran out of ammunition they picked up the guns of fallen police officers and used them. After about fifteen minutes the police were routed and the quartet escaped.

After that incident the group disappeared. Morrell realised later that they had headed north into Canada but at the time she wasn't too interested in where they had gone. She was facing an internal Bureau investigation into the 'Tacoma incident', an investigation that could see her dismissed from the FBI. After a lengthy hearing, Sam wasn't fired, simply because there were sixteen other reports from other law-enforcement officers who said exactly what Sam had said:

Despite being continually gunned down the women just got back up again and returned fire.

The FBI bosses didn't want to hear that, didn't even want to contemplate what that could imply and so the whole affair was quietly swept under the carpet, ignored. Sam was still leading the investigation, although with no new killings and no new leads the case was now on standby. However, her reputation as a rising star within the Bureau was now tarnished, but she was grateful for that—it meant that she could get on with her job without distractions. One piece of information from Tacoma that gave her chills was that the authorities had discharged over two and a half thousand rounds of ammunition during the gunfight.

Gunfight? That was more on the scale of a small war!

The group remained off Sam's radar for eighteen months and during that time she solved a number of other cases, but that did nothing to raise her in the eyes of her colleagues. She would forever be known as the person singularly responsible for 'That Fuck-up in Tacoma'. It was only said to her face once and she slugged the agent for it; from then on she was avoided, a pariah. Eight years on she was still pursuing them and still an object of ridicule within the Bureau. That last caused her to feel bitter because, unlike her colleagues, she *knew* what was going on here. But what would their reaction be if they knew what she did?

Probably even more ridicule because they simply wouldn't believe it.

Chapter 3

Sam arrived in Albuquerque in record time and headed straight for the FBI offices there. As she walked through the offices the agents there pointedly ignored her; she ignored them in return and went to an empty desk. She was just setting herself up when a voice sounded behind her.

'Special Agent Morrell?'

'That's me,' replied Sam. She turned to see an auburn-haired, pretty woman in her early twenties who was dressed in a very smart trouser suit.

'I'm Agent Louise Brody,' said the woman, extending her hand.

'Glad to meet you, Agent Brody,' said Sam, shaking the hand. 'What can I do for you?'

'I've been assigned as your partner,' said Louise.

'Oh,' was all Sam could say. This was the *last* thing in the world she was expecting. Who in the Bureau would *want* to partner her? She gave Brody a level gaze and demanded, 'Who did you piss off to get lumbered with me?'

'Nobody,' replied Brody with a surprised look. 'I requested it.'

Sam was incredulous, not to mention suspicious. In the past her 'colleagues' in the Bureau had tried to set her up on more than one occasion although her sharp instincts as a detective had enabled her to sniff them out. This one was different though, possibly even genuine.

31

'Why the hell would you want to partner me?' Sam demanded.

'Well I . . .' began Louise, but then she stopped when she saw the photo of Chloe Lamont on the desk. 'She's new. Who is she?'

Sam looked down at the photo and replied, 'Her name is Chloe Lamont. She's a resident of a small town east of here called Fulfilment. She was abducted early this morning by the group I'm pursuing.'

'What's your plan of action?' Brody was all business now.

Sam caught the tone of voice and looked closer at Louise. All she could see was a determination to get on with the work and help the case along. Sam was reeling—she wasn't expecting to come within four hours of the group and she wasn't expecting a partner.

'I want to light fires under all law enforcement in at least a three-state radius although I would prefer if the whole country was alerted,' she told Brody.

'I'll get e-mailing while you follow up on the phone?' suggested Louise.

'Sounds good to me,' said Sam. 'Welcome aboard, Agent Brody.'

Brody immediately got to work and scanned the photo they had of Chloe Lamont into the computer. She then added to that the e-fit of Maggie O'Hearn and the artist's impressions of the other two women and began e-mailing them to every police department in the country, from coast to coast, the Mexican border to the Canadian border. Obviously there was more urgency to the notices sent to the police in the surrounding states but Morrell felt it prudent to notify *everybody* to be on the lookout just in case. She knew how quickly and how far this group could move when they chose to.

While Brody was e-mailing, Morrell took upon herself the much harder task of following up those electronic messages with phone calls so she could stress the precautions more fully. It got a bit frustrating at times.

'No, no, no, Sheriff! If you do happen to locate the vehicle they're in then do *not* try and apprehend them!'

'Lieutenant, I appreciate that you are overstretched at the moment. All I'm asking is that if you *should* see them then . . .'

'Captain, I've been following this group for some time now. I know that they're not even near your jurisdiction at the moment but they could so easily be tomorrow night . . .'

'Sergeant, I don't care what kind of *bullshit* you may have heard about me but I am an active agent of the FBI actively working on a live investigation. This group I'm pursuing needs to be brought to book and I need the co-operation of local law enforcement in order to do that. So quit being an asshole and be a policeman!'

'That Fuck-up in Tacoma' had long ago spread into police departments, which meant that her pursuit of this group was made even harder by them not taking her seriously.

By the evening Morrell and Brody had personally alerted the state police in New Mexico, Arizona, Texas, Colorado, Oklahoma, Arkansas, Missouri and Kansas that this group could very well be within their jurisdictions. They had also notified most of the major police departments within those states as well. Morrell wasn't too disheartened; fully half of the departments she had spoken to had taken her seriously and said that they would definitely keep an eye out. It was Chloe Lamont who was having this effect—she was a pretty girl from the country and having her 'held captive' by a group of such vicious desperados motivated the forces more effectively than just having this group killing in their area.

The sun had now set and Morrell was bushed; she had been running on full throttle all day since realising that she had come within four hours of the group. Brody was looking tired too, although she never complained and stayed diligent at her post. Once all the e-mails had been sent she had helped Sam phone police departments to reinforce what had been sent through the worldwide web. Morrell was impressed, very impressed; Louise Brody had all the makings of a very good agent. Provided she didn't get killed on this case, which was a distinct possibility when you considered what they were going up against.

'Come on, Trooper,' Sam said to Brody. 'We've done all we can for today. Let's wrap this up for the night and go and get something to eat.'

'I hear ya!' replied Brody fervently. 'Pardon my French but I'm fuckin' starvin'!'

Sam laughed at this and said, 'Me too, and seeing as I'm the boss I've decided it's time for us to eat.'

They quickly tidied everything up and then went to a nearby diner. They selected a quiet booth in a far corner and perused the menu over a cup of coffee. After the waitress had left with their orders Sam was about to ask Louise why she had requested to partner her but Brody got in first with her question.

'What exactly happened at Tacoma, Ma'am? The only reason why I ask is because that information's wrapped tighter than a gnat's ass! *No one* can get to it!'

'Ahh, Tacoma,' said Sam quietly. She stared off into the distance for a moment before telling Louise all the salient facts of her case up to and just after the Tacoma incident.

'And the bosses didn't investigate the reports of two and a half thousand rounds of ammo doing nothing to these women?' Louise was totally incredulous.

'No, they didn't,' replied Sam. 'I guess looking into that part might upset their sleep or something. No, they just swept it under the carpet and carried on as if nothing out of the ordinary had happened.'

Louise shook her head in disgust. 'And that was eight years ago?'

'Sure was,' answered Sam. 'Eight years of only me in pursuit. Eight years of these women roaming the country and killing unopposed.'

Just then the waitress returned with their meals, and the two women dropped their conversation to concentrate on filling their stomachs.

Chloe always had vivid dreams and when she awoke she could always remember a large part of them. However, when she awoke that evening she went from unconscious to conscious and was only aware of this by the voices she heard.

'Christ, Maggie! What the fuck were you thinking?' Voice Number One, heavily laden with a French accent, female and rather angry.

'I wasn't thinking,' came the reply and Chloe recognised *that* accent—Maggie O'Hearn.

'Obviously,' said Number One sarcastically. 'Shit! We snatched her in front of witnesses, there will be police pursuit you know!'

'I know that,' replied Maggie. 'And it gets worse. I was seen with her last night by about five people.'

'Fuck! That was sloppy Maggie, real sloppy. Why did you do it?'

'It wasn't intentional,' Maggie protested. 'I didn't plan on turning anyone last night.'

'Yeah? But you did and we snatched her in front of her family!'

'It's okay for you two!' said Maggie with some heat. 'You've got each other but I've been real lonely since I lost Caitlin. When you've been with someone as long as I was with her then being alone's the worst thing!'

'Why didn't you say something to us, Mags?' This was another voice, also female, only the accent was quite obviously Italian. 'We could have helped you, planned it so that we could take them quietly with no one around.'

'Because I didn't know beforehand,' answered Maggie. 'I just suddenly realised that I wanted her as my partner and so I nipped her.'

'How did you meet up with her?' asked Number One.

'I was just strolling down the main street and there she was, this pretty blonde girl with lovely eyes, just standing like a statue staring at me.'

There was a deep, despairing sigh from Number One and a quiet chuckle from Number Two, who said, 'You mesmerised her, Mags.'

'I didn't mean to,' protested Maggie.

'I know,' agreed Number Two. 'But you were obviously desperate for a partner and so you cruised for one on full allure. I wondered why you left the bar so early.'

'Why her though?' asked Number One. Her tone was now one of interest.

'She has a real spark in her,' said Maggie.

'A lot of teenagers do,' said Number Two. 'I remember what you were like when you were that age.'

'Yeah,' said Maggie. 'There was just something extra about her. Once I got talking with her I realised that that spark was slowly being eroded by where she was living and the fact that she had no real prospects.'

'I suspect that's an all-too-common story,' commented Number One.

'Anyway,' continued Maggie, 'I took her out into the night, I wanted to see if I could get her to feel a little bit of what we take for granted, give her something a little special to cheer her up.' Maggie paused for a moment and her voice then became really animated. 'She was able to connect with the night almost immediately! She spent

36

hours delighting in it; I've never met anyone with an affinity like hers before. So I asked her if she really wanted to leave where she was and come with me. She said yes, so I nipped her.'

'And then she ran off,' said Number Two.

'Yeah,' said Maggie in a depressed tone. 'I would have run after her, only I had lost track of time out there and I'm normally more aware than that. I noticed that it was very close to sunup so I came and got you.'

'And dropped a real nightmare on us!' hissed Number One.

There was silence for a few moments and then Chloe heard Maggie say, 'I'm sorry, I really fucked up with this one. The police will definitely be looking for her and that puts us all in danger.' She paused, took a deep breath and then continued, 'Tell you what, I'll take Chloe with me and we'll head off on our own. Any police pursuit will be to find her and that'll leave you two safe.'

'No way!' said Voice Number Two, her tone conveying real alarm. 'Maggie, we've been together a long time now and if you were to leave, and over this, then that would make me real sad. We stick together, that's the way it's always been for us. Yes, this could turn dangerous but we'll make it through easier if we're together.'

'She's right,' agreed Voice Number One. 'Although I'm extremely pissed at you for dumping us in this situation there's no way I'm going to let you leave because of it, as that'd *really* upset me. We stick together, we always have and we always will.' And then there was the sound of a kiss being exchanged. Then Chloe heard another sound, of someone inhaling deeply through their nose.

'She's awake,' Number Two said simply.

'Chloe,' said Voice Number One. 'Open your eyes and sit up, we know you're awake.'

Chloe considered lying there and feigning sleep but she

rejected that; they had already sensed that she was aware so what was the use in pretending? Besides, Voice Number One didn't sound very friendly and she didn't want to make her any angrier. She opened her eyes and levered herself up on her elbows. The sight that greeted her was a little eerie but felt in no way threatening. She was lying on the floor of the Winnebago into which she had been snatched that morning; the bus's internal lamps lighted the interior with a warm, suffused glow and the light glistened off the tinfoil that covered all but a small strip of the windshield. The small strip looked to be covered by some sort of tinted film. Up by the driver's cockpit were three people. Maggie O'Hearn, still in her denims, was sitting on a bench-seat-cum-bed just behind the driver's seat. The other two were also women who looked to be about the same age as Maggie. One of them, clad in a black leather jacket, black leather trousers and black leather boots, was sitting sideways in the driver's seat and leaning against the backrest. She was blonde-haired but unlike Maggie she wore her hair fairly short and styled, and her features were more angular than Maggie's too. Although she looked very attractive, she looked like she would be *really* beautiful when she was looking stern.

The second woman, wearing a long, tan-coloured trench coat and what looked like a man's shirt and slacks, wore her deep, coppery-red hair long and she regarded Chloe with a stern, faintly unfriendly expression that was nevertheless beautiful.

'Welcome, Chloe,' said Maggie.

'Who are you people?' Chloe asked in a timid voice. She had heard most of the conversation and was baffled as well as scared because she knew these women were foreign but didn't know why they had snatched her.

'Well,' said the redhead and Chloe knew that this was the Frenchwoman. She indicated herself with her right hand

and continued, 'I'm Jen Albery and . . .' She then laid her hand affectionately on Maggie's shoulder. 'I believe you already know Maggie here. And this . . .' She turned to the woman who was sitting in the driver's seat of the bus.

'I'm Isabella Contracelli,' said the other woman with an Italian accent and a warm smile. 'My friends call me Isa.'

'What do I call you?' asked Chloe, lowering her eyes to the floor of the bus.

'Call me Isa!' the woman said with a laugh.

'Maggie, Jen, Isa,' said Chloe, looking up at them. 'Please, can I go home?'

Jen and Isa turned their attention to Maggie; she turned to face Chloe and said, 'Chloe, your home is with us now, remember what I said to you last night? I could take you away from your dull life but you'd have to let go of everything that had gone before. I meant exactly that, everything. Your home, your family, your friends . . . that shitty factory job in Tucumcari. All that's behind you now, what you've got ahead of you is what's important. The past? Let go of it, none of that matters anymore.'

'Look, my momma's gonna be worried real sick about me, I have to go back!'

'Chloe,' began Maggie, 'think back to this morning when you were heading home. Do you remember how you felt?'

Chloe certainly did and she nodded unhappily.

'How did you feel?' asked Isa.

'Hot and feverish at first,' replied Chloe. 'Weak, I could hardly stand on my own two feet. As I got near my house I felt like I was burnin', literally burnin'. I could even smell my hair singein'.'

'That was the sun doing that,' said Jen. 'And you were lucky this morning as the sun had only just risen. Had you been out later on in the day you would have caught fire and after a couple of minutes you'd have exploded. We only got to you just in time as it was.'

Chloe's eyes widened in alarm at this. 'What are you saying?'

'What we're saying, honey,' said Maggie in a gentle voice after half-scowling at Jen, 'is that daylight is forever denied to you now. To go out in it will kill you. You're like us now, a creature of the night.'

The implications of what Maggie was saying struck Chloe like hammer blows. 'What did you do to me?' she demanded.

Maggie gazed evenly at Chloe and said in a level voice, 'You know.'

'Yeah,' replied Chloe in an unfriendly tone. 'You bit m . . .' And her hand shot to her neck.

Despite education in rural New Mexico not being the best, both Chloe and her sister had been very studious as children. As a result they had gleaned a lot of knowledge during their school years and understanding of what had happened to her dawned on Chloe *very* quickly.

'Jesus. Fuckin'. Aitch. Christ!' said Chloe in a choked whisper, scuttling backwards with her eyes as wide as saucers. She regarded the three women with fear and loathing.

'I suppose it's natural enough to be horrified by what we are,' said Maggie matter-of-factly. 'But Chloe,' she leaned forward, 'you have absolutely no reason to be scared of us, we're your sisters now, we're kin and we stand together.'

Isa reinforced this with a stern nod. Jen continued staring darkly at the teenager.

'How did you know what I was feeling?' demanded Chloe; that they could read her so easily was a little scary. It made her feel like she could have nothing truly her own.

Maggie gave a quiet little laugh, sat back in her seat and said, 'I've been around for quite some time now and when you've lived as long as I have, reading people becomes second nature. Together with the fact that you

40

youngsters do have a tendency to wear your hearts on your sleeves.'

Isa snorted at this and added, 'I can see why Maggie was so drawn to you.' She turned to her friend and said, 'You're right, Mags, this girl does have some real spark in her, I can see it even now.' She turned a friendly, welcoming look on Chloe and said, 'She'll be a welcome addition.'

'We'll see,' said Jen, her accent making this non-committal comment musical. 'Our first order of business is to get moving and change vehicles. There are a lot of beaten-up Winnebagos on the road, but why chance getting spotted by a cop when we don't have to?'

'Besides,' said Maggie, 'we've been in this vehicle a bit longer than we should have, ditching it is a sensible precaution in any case.'

'That settles it then,' said Jen. 'Let's get moving.'

And with that, Isa swung herself around so that she was sitting properly in the driver's seat and fired the engine up. As the ignition caught the whole bus vibrated and there was an alarming knocking sound from the engine.

'Damn thing's fuckin' noisy, that's for sure!' Isa muttered sourly. 'We'll be well shot of this old banger!' This elicited fond smiles from both Jen and Maggie.

Chloe was still lying on the floor propped up by her elbows; Maggie indicated the bench-seat she was sitting on by patting the vacant space next to her. Although Chloe was still reeling from what had happened, was frightened witless actually, she could clearly see that Maggie meant her no harm. So she got to her feet and went to sit beside the woman. As Chloe sat down, Maggie put an arm around her shoulders and pulled her a bit closer. The simple, honest warmth of that action soothed Chloe's nerves some and she leaned into Maggie's embrace. Maggie completed it by resting her cheek on the top of Chloe's head.

41

Chloe saw Jen glance at them and saw the gentle smile that flickered briefly across the woman's lips. Chloe wasn't sure what to make of this as her first impression of Jen was that the redhead didn't like her.

They travelled in silence for about five minutes until Chloe couldn't contain her curiosity any more and asked, 'Isabella Contracelli?'

'Yeah?' said Isa back over her shoulder.

'You're Italian?' Chloe ventured.

'Sure am,' replied Isa. 'I'm originally from the Tuscany region of Italy although that was . . . some time ago.'

Jen and Maggie quietly laughed at this, and the way Isa had said 'some time ago' was exactly the same way Maggie had said those words the night before. Chloe wondered just how old these women actually were.

'And Jen is . . .?' began Chloe.

'Is Jen,' interrupted the red-haired woman with finality. Chloe jerked back at the shortness of her answer.

'Pah!' scoffed Isa and said back over her shoulder to Chloe, 'Jen is actually *Geneviève Albiére, he-hoh-he-hoh.*' She put on a clichéd French accent when she said the name and, mixed with her strong Italian accent, it almost sounded hilarious. 'She was once a member of a minor noble family from near Bordeaux in France. *'owever. . .*' Clichéd French accent again. 'She gave up being a stuck-up, posh broad in favour of being a *stuck-up, scruffy drifter.*'

Maggie barked a laugh at this.

'*'ey! Fucka you and the 'orse you roda in on, you greasy Wop!*' Jen shot back in an equally clichéd Italian accent.

Chloe was a bit startled by the barbs the two women were hurling at each other but all Isa did was throw her head back and laugh hard. The fond look on Maggie's face told Chloe that Jen and Isa had a very close relationship. So close that they could barrack and tease one another merci- lessly, safe in the knowledge that what they said to each other would not damage their relationship in any way. In fact, it would only strengthen it.

'You really from Boston?' Chloe asked Maggie, who regarded her fondly and replied, 'Oh yes, you and I are true Americans, unlike these two immigrants.' She inclined her head towards Jen and Isa.

Isa's only reply was a raspberry and all Jen did was give Maggie the finger. Maggie just stuck her tongue out at them in reply. Chloe was still very uncertain about the situation although she felt very comfortable in Maggie's embrace. She looked up at the woman, who gave her a gentle smile. Chloe knew that she had no problems with Maggie and Isa seemed friendly enough as well. Chloe realised that Jen could be troublesome although that little smile she gave and the relationship she had with both Isa and Maggie indicated a deep warmth in the woman. The situation she was in was no longer scary but it certainly was surreal. One question that was bugging her, though, was where the hell was she?

'Where are we anyway?' she asked them, hoping that it wouldn't get her an angry response.

'We're just leaving Tucumcari,' replied Isa in a friendly, conversational tone as though the four of them were just out for a drive. 'And heading for ... where we headed, Jen?'

Jen looked at a road map and replied, 'Dumas, northwest Texas. We'll decide which way we go and pick up a new vehicle when we're there.'

Chloe turned to Maggie and asked quietly, 'What happens now?'

'We introduce you to your new life,' answered Maggie with a broad smile. 'We've told you the drawbacks of how we live—can't stand the sun or be with your family. Now we're gonna show you the benefits.'

'What do we do?' asked Chloe.

Maggie touched her nose to Chloe's and said, 'Anything we want, sweetheart, until the end of time.'

Until the end of time. Those five words brought home to Chloe just how profoundly her life had changed. She knew what these women were, what she was now.

Funny thing was, this didn't scare her at all.

'Cool,' she said.

Jen raised her eyebrows at that.

Chapter 4

During the eighteen-month period of quiet following Tacoma, Sam had delved into police files from all over the country regarding unsolved multiple murders. Although she had no proof to link any of these particular killings to the group of women she was chasing, a number of the murders nevertheless had all the hallmarks associated with them. The trouble was that Morrell was finding cases from as far back as 1950 that bore similarities to the killings carried out by these four women.

When did they start?

It was a question that Sam wasn't able to answer at that time, but she kept plugging away, trying to find more clues about this group. Diligent. Relentless.

Sam was also a studious woman outside of her work for the FBI and had developed a passion for American history. America was probably the most powerful country in the world but also ranked among one of the youngest—the Declaration of Independence was only ratified in 1783 when Europe was already well into middle age. So Sam spent much of her downtime trawling through various history texts to give herself a much clearer picture of what exactly had originally founded the USA. It was in one of these history books that Morrell made a discovery that would help her with the case.

A rather disturbing discovery.

One of the key cities in the founding of the USA was Boston, Massachusetts and Sam was reading an account of an Irish-immigrant couple who had landed there in 1798. Within two years of arriving, Patrick O'Hearn had established a very successful import/export business, bringing in English tea, Irish whiskey and Chinese silks and sending back beaver furs and tobacco. In 1804 his wife, Megan, gave birth to a daughter whom they christened Margaret. Three sons followed in the next eight years and the O'Hearns became a minor celebrity family due to Patrick's business success. In 1822, when she was just eighteen, Margaret, or Maggie as she was more commonly known, vanished. She disappeared three days before she was due to be married and was never seen again by family or friends. The history book contained a portrait, painted by a now-forgotten artist, of the entire O'Hearn family prior to Maggie's disappearance. Patrick and Megan were standing proud at the back and ranged in front of them were their sons, Patrick junior, Sean and Robert. However, it was the person standing next to Patrick senior that gave Morrell goosebumps—eighteen-year-old Maggie O'Hearn.

She looked like a younger version of one of the four women that Sam had desperately tried to gun down in Tacoma some fourteen months previously.

A descendent perhaps? There certainly was a *very* uncanny likeness. However, what Sam was looking at was a painting, so she then decided to try something. She scanned the portrait into the Bureau's computer system and then 'aged' the face of Maggie so that she looked in her mid-thirties. To Morrell the e-fit picture she had produced looked almost exactly like one of the quartet. She needed a second opinion and so she printed the e-fit photo and went to the only other surviving agent from the Tacoma operation and showed him. Paul Jeffson didn't want anything to do with Morrell—he personally blamed her for the debacle of that night—but she wouldn't desist and ended up shoving the picture under his nose. When he saw the photo he studied it for a few moments, looked Morrell in the eye and said, 'Yup, that's one of them.'

She knew Jeffson, he was definitely a no bullshit character and if he said, 'Yup, that's one of them' then you could pretty much take it to the bank.

Obviously Sam thought that she was mistaken as to the identity as she was only going on a portrait of an eighteen-year-old girl. A one-hundred-and-seventy-year-old portrait. Yet despite it going against her training and her natural scepticism, Sam was pretty sure that one of the quartet *was* Maggie O'Hearn.

But that would mean that Maggie was over one hundred and eighty years old.

That, of course, was impossible! Then Morrell thought back to the one horrifying fact of that gunfight in Tacoma that everybody conveniently ignored: all four women refused to die despite being shot literally hundreds of times. Maggie, it seemed, was unkillable, so a prolonged lifespan wasn't completely out of the question.

But one hundred and eighty something and still look only in her mid-thirties?

Morrell decided that one was pure chance but two would be more convincing, and so she then plunged headlong into the national database on missing persons. When she wasn't working on other cases she would delve into the missing-persons database and go through countless files. Week upon week was spent poring through photographs of women who had simply vanished without a trace down through the years. It was slow, painstaking, frustrating work. But it paid off.

Four months after starting her search, Sam finally found a photograph of a woman who looked like a younger version of another member of the quartet. She put it through the computer and produced another e-fit photo that she had 'aged'. Then she sought out Paul Jeffson again. Knowing that he didn't like her, she just walked up to him and showed him the new e-fit picture. He looked at it carefully, looked Morrell in the eye, nodded and said, 'Yup, that's another one.'

Morrell nodded and walked away; she had identified another of the group, Caitlin Baker. She was born in 1890 in Minneapolis, Minnesota and had vanished in 1910. The photo Morrell had found was the last one ever taken of her, on her twentieth birthday. She had disappeared four days later.

Two women, one born in 1890 and the other in 1804. Still alive?

Under normal circumstances Morrell would have dismissed this immediately, but there was a problem. These women could not be shot dead. Because of this she was beginning to accept, in theory at least, that these two women were incredibly old. But how were they able to live for so long and still look youthful? If she could answer that one then she would probably be able to answer the really big question: why couldn't two and a half thousand rounds of ammunition kill them?

It was at that time that the quartet came back on the radar: a multiple killing in Gregory, South Dakota. Morrell immediately went back into action and contacted all law enforcement between Gregory and the Canadian border to find out whether there were any other multiple murders recently. The answer was no, but in Bismarck, North Dakota four individuals had been murdered in separate incidents, though the killings all bore similarities to the killings carried out by this group. Fortune was smiling on Morrell this time; there were witnesses in Gregory and Bismarck who had seen four women arrive in their towns in vehicles that later turned out to be stolen. She immediately travelled to

48

Gregory and Bismarck to interview the witnesses and she took with her the two e-fit photos plus the artist's impressions she had of the other two women. When shown the four pictures, the witnesses swore blind that they were the strangers they had seen.

The quartet were most definitely back.

Morrell was determined to nail them this time. She tried to arrange, like she did before, a network of communication throughout all the police departments in middle America to locate and track the group. It was then that she discovered that her *fame*, 'That Fuck-up in Tacoma', had spread beyond the FBI.

Numerous departments didn't take her requests seriously or report any multiple killings to her. Despite repeated communications with state and regional departments, Sam received very little in the way of information. She had a very hard time tracking the group's movements and it was only by going to the areas where killings had occurred and speaking with law enforcement in person that she got any leads.

The group had been back for six months and because of the lack of communication, Sam could only guess at the death toll. Bismarck had informed her that they didn't just kill groups of people as a group, they killed singly too. It wasn't until a sheriff from Brunswick, Missouri contacted her that she was able to finally realise something about this group. Something that would answer both of her questions, about their age and their seeming invulnerability.

The sheriff reported to her a single murder that had taken place in his town. The reason why he was reporting this single killing was that one of the four women, Caitlin Baker, had been seen in Brunswick around the time the victim disappeared. However, it was the pathologist's report on the victim that contained the real prize piece of information for Morrell:

The victim died from extreme blood loss caused by a wound in her jugular vein. The wound was caused by a bite that could only have been made by <u>human</u> teeth.

It clicked together then. A very long series of killings by a group that were seen only at night. They, apparently, had very long life spans and they were bullet-proof.

What that said to Morrell, taken with the clue from the Brunswick killing, scared her and scared her badly. These women weren't murdering.

They were feeding.

O'Hearn and Baker *were* those women she had found from a century or more ago. The reason she wasn't able to identify the other two members? Because they were probably older than Maggie and Caitlin and they had probably come here from Europe.

It didn't make the case any easier for Morrell, in fact it made it a lot, lot harder. She didn't feel she could share this with anyone, they'd just think she was crazy and she'd either be shuffled off the case and into some department where she would cause least harm, or be shipped off to an asylum. So Sam undertook a mission to hunt them down and destroy them on her own; it was a lonely and frustrating time for her as she received very little in the way of support. But she persevered and five years later she had some success—she managed, finally, to kill one of them: Caitlin Baker. The other three eluded her, however.

A year on and Sam was hot on their trail again and she was determined to finish it this time. She knew what they were and, more importantly, she now knew how to kill them.

*

50

After a rather filling steak dinner and an equally filling dessert of apple pie and cream, Morrell and Brody were sitting quietly and letting their dinner digest. Sam was drinking yet another cup of coffee and normally would have cursed herself, as that much caffeine would cause her not to sleep. Not tonight though, she could feel her eyelids getting heavier by the minute. But before she went to sleep there was something she needed to know.

'So come on, Louise. I'm itching to know why you, a cherry new agent, would request to be partnered with the FBI's most unwanted?'

Brody gave a small smile, collected her thoughts and said 'I grew up in Cochise, a small town some sixty miles east of Tucson, Arizona. You know, I've always wanted to be a federal agent, ever since I was a little girl.' She shrugged self-deprecatingly. 'I know it's a bit idealistic and starry-eyed.'

'Don't worry,' replied Sam. 'I won't snigger at you. This country's going to hell in a handbasket, so we need more idealistic young men and women like you to join law enforcement.'

'Anyway,' continued Brody, 'I signed up for the Bureau, passed the entrance exam and then underwent training at Quantico. It was while I was there that I began to hear stories about this agent called Samantha Morrell. Whispers in corridors about how incompetent she was and how she got fifty policemen killed one night.'

'Fifty?' exclaimed Morrell. 'Christ! The number gets bigger with every re-telling. It was only twenty-one killed and four of them were FBI agents. What's more, it wasn't my fault, how could anybody have known that bullets couldn't kill these women? That doesn't matter though, everybody wants to blame me so they blame me!'

'Yeah, anyway, I'm from rural Arizona but country don't

mean dumb. If you were that bad then the Bureau would have fired you, so I guessed there was more to the story than what the rumours were saying. So I began looking into the infamous Sam Morrell.' She looked across to Sam.

'And what did you find, Agent Brody?' Sam asked with a raised eyebrow.

'Something that took me right back to my childhood,' Louise replied. 'When I was eight years old four people were murdered just on the outskirts of town one night. There was an old guy that lived there, still does actually, called Mort Larney. Now everyone in town considered him crazy, but I didn't, that old guy doesn't miss a trick. He's well into his nineties now, so back then he was at least eighty but still sharp as a tack. On the night of those murders he claimed to have seen four strangers, women, around the area where the killings took place. He then claimed that the four women he saw that night looked exactly the same as four women he saw some seventy or so years previously when another multiple killing took place in the town. Everyone dismissed him of course—even I did on hearing that—but when I read about your case I thought of him. And then I did something really naughty.' She gave Morrell a tight grin.

'And what did you do, Agent Brody?' asked Sam, still with a raised eyebrow and the corners of her mouth now twitching upward.

'I printed off copies of the e-fits and the artist's impressions that you had of these women and when I next went home I took them with me,' replied Brody.

'And you showed them to this Mort Larney.' Sam was stating, not questioning.

Brody just nodded.

'What did he say, Louise?'

'"That's 'em, Lou,"' said Brody with a thick accent. '"That's 'em wimmin who did those killins some fourteen years back. And the killins that took place when I was a boy seventy years ago." '

'What did you think when he said that?' asked Morrell.

'I thought "Shit!" That's what I thought!' exclaimed Brody. 'Four women who haven't aged in, and have been killing for, some eighty years or so. They're only seen at night, if at all, and now I learn you can't kill them with bullets. I didn't like what all that suggested.'

'And what did it suggest to you, Agent Brody?'

Louise was silent for a few moments before answering, 'I didn't know what it suggested exactly. I only knew that I didn't like it. It wasn't until I read the Brunswick pathologist's report in your case file a couple of days ago that the penny finally dropped for me.'

There was silence for a minute until Morrell quietly said, 'Please say it, Louise.'

'They're vampires.'

There it was, finally! Someone saying out loud what Sam had known for six years. The relief she felt was enormous, and she let out a huge sigh.

'How long have you been alone with this, Ma'am?'

'Six years,' Sam replied. 'And call me Sam from now on.'

'Six years? With no support?'

'I had support but I had to request it in very broad terms,' said Morrell. 'I had to be very careful of what I said otherwise I'd get hauled off to the nearest booby hatch. That posed its own problems, though, because many local lawboys couldn't understand my order that if the group was discovered at night then we were to maintain surveillance at a distance. When I told them it was for their own protection they just sneered at me, considered me a faint-hearted woman who was in way over her head!' Sam couldn't hide the contempt or the bitterness from her voice. 'The last six years have been among the loneliest of my life.'

'You've had positive sightings of them on the road?' asked Brody. This was news to her.

'Oh God, yes!' answered Morrell with some fervour. 'There've been numerous sightings down through the years. The trouble was the sightings were always a few days old, which meant that they were long gone from wherever it was they were seen by the time I heard about it. I've been trying to shag their butts ever since they came back from Canada but because of the difficulties I've had within the Bureau and not being able to say outright what we're up against, I've never been able to close on them properly. I've been effectively hamstrung by my own side all this time.'

'You managed to close right in on them last year, though, didn't you?' Brody pointed out.

'Caitlin Baker,' Sam murmured. 'That was more luck than anything else,' she admitted. 'They were a little careless with the kills they'd made in Alliance, Nebraska. I was in Scottsbluff just to the southwest at the time and I received the call the next morning. Good sheriff in Alliance, I forget his name now, but when he found the bodies he called me first thing and told me. I had a look at the map and saw that I was close and maybe, just maybe, they'd gone to ground in Scottsbluff. So I had a good nose around the town and sink me! I found it.'

'Found what?' asked Brody.

'The vehicle they were travelling in, a Ford Liberty I think it was.'

'How did you know it was their vehicle?' asked Brody.

'Because it had been darkened,' replied Morrell.

'Darkened?' Louise was puzzled.

'Yeah, think about it. You can't abide sunlight and if you're going to sleep the day in something that could be exposed to sunlight, like a windowed vehicle, well, you need to block those windows. These girls use tinfoil mostly but they'll also use blankets, plastic bags, cardboard or anything

54

else to make the interior free of sunlight. Hence my term "darkened".'

'They even put tinfoil on the windshield?'

'Yup.'

'How'd they see out?'

'They leave a strip about eight inches wide at eye level.' Sam pantomimed the strip with her hands. 'They cover that bit with tinted plastic—you know, the kind you use for a sunstrip at the top of the windshield. They do the same with the bottom corners of the front windows so that they can see the side mirrors.'

'So they can move around during the day?' Brody was surprised at this.

'If they have to they can,' replied Morrell. 'But they usually bed down before dawn. None of the sightings that I've been told about have ever taken place during the hours of daylight.'

'Until this morning,' said Brody.

'Yeah, they took a hell of a risk doing that. Snatching Chloe in front of her family can only mean one thing.'

'What?'

Morrell's voice was dead flat when she answered, 'Chloe's already been turned. She's lost to us now.'

Sam bade her partner—her *partner*! She was still reeling from the fact that she finally had an ally—good night in the parking lot of a nearby motel. It seemed to Sam that she spent most of her nights sleeping in motels, whether it was New Mexico or New Hampshire. In her darker hours Morrell got to thinking that she wouldn't resolve this case until she had slept in *every* motel in America at least once. As she lay in bed waiting for sleep to claim her she wondered what Chloe was doing right now; the girl would certainly be up and moving, but would she be killing, feeding for herself?

Sam didn't think so; she reasoned that it would take some time to overcome your natural repulsion to doing something like that. Sam bit back a few tears that were threatening to brim over; Chloe was only seventeen and hadn't done anything wrong in her life up until now, but Sam was going to have to kill her along with the other three.

Chapter 5

The four women reached Dumas rather quickly due to no traffic and Jen's urgent demand that they switch vehicles as soon as possible. Isa found a stand of trees behind a disused factory on the town's outskirts to dump the Winnebago in. Chloe was impressed with the speed with which these women moved; as soon as the bus stopped Jen was jumping out of it and turning to catch a holdall that Maggie threw after her. Isa tore away the tinfoil from the windshield and side windows. She saved the strips of tinted film but crumpled the rest up into a ball. She put the window tint into another, smaller bag, then followed Jen out of the door. Maggie picked up another small bag and then headed out the door herself, propelling Chloe in front of her. Outside the bus, Chloe didn't even have time to get her bearings before they were walking through the quiet night at a fair pace, Jen first, looking at the road map, followed by Isa, with Maggie and herself bringing up the rear.

'What kinda wheels?' Isa asked Jen.

'Any kind,' replied Jen. 'We'll only use it to take us to the next town. There we'll feed and get ourselves something suitable for a long haul.'

'Long haul?' queried Maggie. 'Where are we headed?'

'Haven't decided yet, but I want to head northward and put some distance between us and *her* hometown.' She half-scowled at Chloe, who shrank back against Maggie.

Maggie growled. 'Ease up Jen, will ya? It's only her first night for Christ's sake!'

'I wouldn't be pushing us like this if I felt we had the luxury of time but at the moment we do not!' Jen snapped back. 'Remember, Maggie, we snatched her in front of witnesses, the police will be looking for her!'

'I'm aware of that but taking it out on her is only going to cause bad feelings between the two of you and we can't have that in the group. It'll split us up in the end and I'd hate that.'

'She's right, Jen,' said Isa quietly. 'And we can't start arguing now otherwise our guard will drop and we could easily get a repeat of what happened to Caitlin.'

'I'm still trying to figure out how that happened,' grumbled Jen.

'Easy,' replied Maggie in a subdued tone. 'We got careless and the cops were able to find where we were sleeping. They opened the van to daylight in trying to arrest us.'

'I'm hoping that's all it was,' said Jen with all seriousness. 'Because the one factor that has enabled us to move with ease through the country all these years is the modern person's refusal to believe in the likes of us. If someone cottons on to what we truly are and believes it then we're going to have no peace. We'll be hunted from coast to coast until we're found and dragged into the sunlight, and I don't much fancy that!'

'That makes four of us,' commented Isa. 'But Maggie's right, Jen, stop taking this out on Chloe—after all, she didn't have any choice in joining us.' And she mockingly wagged a stern finger at Maggie. All Maggie could do was shrug her shoulders in a 'so sue me' gesture.

They carried on in silence until they found a street, near the industrial part of town, which contained some cars. One of the cars was a brand new Dodge Viper.

'Don't even think it, Isa!' said Jen sternly, her expression matching her voice.

'Aw come on!' pleaded Isa in a mocking way as she ran her hand over the car's sleek lines. 'I've always wanted to drive one of these puppies.'

'We steal that and we'll have *everyone* on our ass! Let's find something a little less conspicuous.' Jen couldn't hide the fond, loving smile she had for Isa though.

The next two cars were rejected as they were pick-up trucks—you could squeeze four into them but you would have to *squeeze*.

'This'll do,' said Isa, referring to the next car, a Chevy Ford. It was quite old and the bodywork had rusted away in some places; it was a colour that Chloe could only describe as 'crappy blue'.

'Yeah, this'll do,' said Jen. 'We'll use this to get to . . .' And she referred to the map while Isa fished a coat hanger out of her bag and set about opening the car. 'Dalhart,' continued Jen. 'It's the only large settlement directly to the north, the rest look to be a lot smaller and I don't want to risk feeding in any of them. However, I don't want to be in Dalhart for any longer than an hour, so it's feed quickly, find a vehicle quickly and hit the road again.'

'Gotcha!' said Maggie, hauling open the door and climbing into the back with Chloe.

Jen climbed into the front passenger seat while Isa got behind the wheel and hot-wired the ignition. The car coughed into life with a loud rattle.

'Why do I always pick the noisy ones?' Isa grumbled to herself and then put the car into first gear and pulled away.

Within ten minutes of arriving in Dumas they had switched vehicles and were now leaving the town and heading northwest to Dalhart.

Chloe had stayed silent throughout all this, firstly because she was still a little unsure of where she fitted in with this group but also because she was starting to feel a bit queer. *Queer*, that was the only way she could describe it; she felt both light-headed and leaden. Her head ached and her body pulsed from hot to cold in a regular, slow rhythm. Maggie didn't notice anything was up until Chloe began to shiver like someone about to have a fit.

'What's up, hon?' she asked.

'Don't know,' replied Chloe through chattering teeth. 'I've come over all weird. Feel hot, then cold and my head's turnin' from air to mud an' back again.'

'Shit!' exclaimed Isa. 'She's turning real fast!'

'You're not wrong there, sis,' agreed Maggie. 'This is even quicker than Caitlin.'

'Isa,' said Jen quietly, 'get us to Dalhart as quickly as possible but don't attract any attention.'

'You got it,' replied Isa.

'It's okay, sweetheart,' Maggie told Chloe with a reassuring smile and a comforting hand on the girl's brow. 'You're just hungry, that's all.'

'Can't we stop for a burger then?' Chloe asked with all earnestness.

There was a thunderstruck silence in the car for a few moments before Jen, Isa and Maggie all burst out laughing.

'"Can't we stop for a burger then?"' Isa chortled. 'Man, someone write that down, that one's fuckin' priceless!'

After a couple of minutes the three women got their mirth under control and it was then that Isa saw, in the interior mirror, Chloe's sly grin. She turned her head from the road to give the teenager a glowing look.

'Chloe.' Isa practically sang her name. 'You are *so* going to fit in with us.' And then she turned her concentration back to the road.

'What was that about?' Jen demanded.

60

'She was jerking our chain with that burger line,' Isa grinned.

Jen turned a startled expression toward Chloe, who just grinned back impishly. Then the teenager was wracked by shivering again. Maggie enfolded the girl in a massive hug and said, 'Don't worry, once we get to Dalhart I'll see to it.'

'Thank you,' said Chloe, still shivering. 'I don't think I could kill for myself tonight.' The mere thought of it was repugnant beyond belief to her.

'Don't you worry about that,' said Maggie. 'I'll drink deeply and feed you off my wrist. You'll be feeding that way for some time until you learn how to feed yourself.'

'Not too long though,' said Jen darkly. 'She needs to be independent as soon as.'

Both Maggie and Isa scowled at Jen but neither woman said a word; they both knew Jen extremely well and to say anything while she was in this mood would cause a big argument.

The road they were travelling on was practically empty so Isa was able to put her foot to the floor and the women were in Dalhart inside thirty minutes. They ditched the car in a side street and walked down a couple of other streets until they were some distance from the car. There they split up, Isa vanishing into the night saying 'I'll get the wheels.'

'We'll meet back here in an hour,' Jen told Maggie. 'Quicker if you can.'

'Sure thing, Jen,' said Maggie, taking hold of Chloe's hand and leading her away.

Jen stared after the two of them and shook her head. It wasn't that she disliked Chloe, quite the opposite actually. Jen agreed with Isa that Chloe would fit right in—that line about the burger was a good one. No, it was that they had snatched her in front of witnesses, that Maggie had been seen with her. The authorities would certainly be searching for her, which meant possible pursuit. But if anyone linked Chloe's abductors to the killings they had carried out then there would be a full-on pursuit from *all* law enforcement in the country.

Jen shook her head, it was a worry she could well do without, but this was the situation they were in so they'd just have to deal with it. They would have to be on their guard for the next week or so, be prepared to react should anyone come looking for them. But to more pressing matters. Jen then closed her eyes and breathed in deeply of the night air. How many centuries? The high the night gave her had never diminished in all that time. Jen opened her eyes and if anyone had seen the look on her face they would have run for it—she wore the feral look of a hungry predator, out in search of prey. Jen put the holdall over her shoulder and slipped into the night to find a victim to quench her thirst.

'Okay, Chloe,' said Maggie as the two of them walked down a quiet road on the edge of the town centre. 'I'll do the killing but you must watch. A big part of the problem you'll face in making a kill for yourself is overcoming your natural repugnance. By watching me over the next however many nights, hopefully your reluctance will be eroded until you can kill for yourself.'

'Okay,' said Chloe with a large amount of uncertainty.

'Don't worry,' Maggie reassured her. 'When I first came over I was like you are now, convinced that I couldn't kill. Take it from me, we've all gone through it.' She stopped and surveyed the area they were in. They were next to a large single-storey building that looked like it might be a workshop during the day, but now it was silent, closed, the windows as dark as the night. There was a wide alleyway running down one side between the building and a low, bush-topped wall. A pretty good killing ground really. Maggie closed her eyes and let the night fill her. The sights and sounds of the town filled her head but she filtered them all out, she was focusing on one thing only. Warm human blood. Dalhart was fairly large so the pulse of blood boomed in Maggie's mind. She narrowed her focus right down and quickly sensed a solitary person walking towards where they were.

'Chloe, crouch in those bushes over there about halfway down.' She indicated an area atop the wall. 'And keep perfectly still but remember to watch.'

'Okay,' said Chloe. She knew that she could crouch in the bushes all right but could she keep perfectly still while she was shivering like this? She didn't think so but she took the small bag from Maggie and took her place. Once she was in the bushes and viewing Maggie from her vantage point with full knowledge of what Maggie was going to do her shivering immediately abated. A new part of her, a feral part, rose up and calmed her with the promise of warm, sweet blood. Chloe remained in among the dark foliage as immovable as stone.

Maggie's senses told her that a person was approaching but not the gender; she had to use her eyes to determine that. She stayed out of sight until the person got closer. Gender didn't really matter to Maggie as she had been doing this for so long and was adept at luring either sex, but Jen was in a hurry so she hoped that it would be a man approaching—they were *always* easier targets.

Sure enough it was a man. Maggie stepped out of the shadows and then back into them again, a brief flicker of movement designed to catch the eye. It worked, it always did. The man was ambling along the sidewalk, humming a tune to himself when Maggie's movement attracted his attention. His eyes were now on the spot where Maggie was so she now moved slowly and deliberately to let him know she was there. Once she was sure that his attention was firmly fixed on her she stepped partially into the light but turned away from him so that he could catch her face in profile. She then moved the edge of her jacket backwards to reveal the swell of her breast under her white tee shirt. Then she slowly moved back into the dark area and down the alleyway. He was walking on the other side of the street but when he saw Maggie in profile he automatically crossed over, wanting a closer look. She had hooked him, she was reeling him in, and now all that was left to do was land him. She could just kill him as soon as he stepped into the shadows but she wanted Chloe to learn the subtleties of making a kill and so decided to draw it out for her benefit. Maggie stayed in the shadows but kept moving as though she were about some business.

'Hi there!' sounded the man's voice.

'Oh!' Maggie jerked up and feigned surprise. 'You startled me!'

'Sorry, ma'am,' said the man. 'What are you up to?'

Maggie turned to face him fully with her hands on her hips and a smile on her lips.

'Can't a girl have *any* secrets?' she scolded him.

He laughed out loud. 'Depends on what those secrets are,' he said suggestively.

Maggie's smiled broadened and her eyes widened as she said in a husky voice, 'Dirty secrets.'

'Well,' said the man, failing to keep the grin out of his voice. 'I've always found that those secrets are better if they're shared.' And he stepped toward her.

'Is that so?' she replied suggestively and tilted her head back slightly. The man stepped closer again and Maggie reached out and traced her forefinger down the front of his chest. The man shuddered pleasurably, unable to take his eyes from Maggie's as she transfixed him with her gaze.

'I have a *really* dirty secret that I'd dearly love to share with you,' she whispered.

64

'Really,' said the man, his voice hoarse as Maggie stepped closer and nuzzled his cheek.

Chloe had a perfect view of the scene before her and had seen how effectively, how effortlessly Maggie had snared this poor schmuck. From the first quick movement to draw his eye, the slower moves to draw him in and now the word play and hypnotic eye contact to seal his fate. A small part of Chloe desperately wanted to look away but a much larger part was transfixed by the scene playing before her, taking it all in, learning.

Now Maggie was making physical contact with him, lulling him, dulling his senses. She watched as Maggie's soft lips massaged the man's face and neck and then Maggie made direct eye contact with Chloe. This was the moment and Chloe wanted to squeeze her eyes shut but they remained stubbornly open, eager to see the *coup de grâce*. She saw Maggie take a firm hold of the man's head with one hand, clamp the other hand over his mouth and then bite hard into his neck. The man's gargled cry of agony was muted by Maggie's hand and as the blood flowed from his severed vein his life went with it. Maggie kept her mouth firmly clamped to man's neck long after his lifeless body had slumped against her and she didn't release until she had practically drained him. Then she let his body fall to the floor and emitted a long, wet belch that spoke of having overly gorged. She swayed slightly on her feet and her expression went woozy but she was able to bring herself back.

'Damn,' she muttered quietly, wiping the blood from her mouth and chin. 'I'd forgotten how taking that much in one go knocks you sideways.' She then beckoned Chloe out of the shadows and said, 'That's how you feed, straight from the vein. The jugular's the best one although the one in the wrist will feed you just as well.' She then reached into

65

her pocket and as she pulled her hand out she gave a much-practised flick of the wrist and brought out into the open a butterfly knife. Chloe had no doubt that the blade was razor sharp but still winced when Maggie quite deliberately slit his throat from ear to ear; then she casually wiped the blade clean on his clothes.

'Why do you do that?' she asked in a tiny voice.

'Do what?'

'Slit his throat.'

'To hide the bite marks,' replied Maggie. 'You heard Jen say about modern people's refusal to believe that we exist?'

Chloe nodded.

'Why shake that disbelief with clues? Doing this helps protect us, keeps us hidden. Sometimes we'll break the victim's neck and then feed from their wrist although that takes some practice to get right. We then mangle the arm up to the elbow to hide the marks. We do that to someone in a car, make it look like they died in a crash.'

Chloe raised her eyebrows at this; the three women certainly knew how to keep a low profile with their feeding. She then asked, 'What will you do with the body?'

'Dump it someplace where it won't be found for several days. By then we'll be a long ways from here.'

Chloe nodded understanding; it was better than leaving it out in the open. She was then startled when Maggie hoisted the corpse onto her shoulder like it weighed nothing more than a small knapsack. Maggie obviously had amazing strength.

'Does feeding give you that kind of strength?' Chloe asked, her tone reflecting her amazement.

'No, we have this strength all the time, it's part of what we are.'

'Oh,' was all Chloe could say.

Maggie walked down the alley with the man's body over

her shoulder and Chloe in tow; she turned the corner and said, 'Aha.'

She then dropped the man's body to the floor and bent down. Just in front of her was a manhole cover. 'We'll dump his body in here, should take them a while to find it.' And she stuck her fingers into the gaps where workers normally use metal spikes and lifted the heavy cover with no effort whatsoever. She relieved the man of the cash and credit cards in his wallet and then dumped him unceremoniously into the hole before replacing the cover.

'Maggie, do you ever wonder about the people you kill? You know, who they were, what family they had?'

'Does a lion think about such things after it's brought down a zebra?' Maggie countered.

'I guess not,' replied Chloe with sadness.

'Sweetheart,' said Maggie, taking Chloe's face in both hands and gazing deeply into the girl's eyes, 'we are just like lions. We hunt people for their blood because that's what we need in order to survive. Sometimes we kill others who may have seen what we're doing but we only kill them because to leave them alive will threaten our safety. We don't kill just for the sake of it, that's something only humans do.'

Chloe smiled sadly up at Maggie and said, 'It just feels so wrong.'

'Of course it does,' said Maggie. 'You still think of yourself as normal, a human. In time your perspective will change and it won't register on you anymore.' She kissed Chloe's forehead and continued, 'Now, let's get you fed and back to the others and then we can get out of here. Kneel down.'

Chloe did as she was told and looked up at Maggie, who put her wrist to her mouth and bit into it. She then lowered her arm so that the wound was level with Chloe's face. A war began to rage in Chloe at that moment, human revulsion against inhuman hunger. The hunger won out, and Chloe leant forward and began to lick the wound in Maggie's wrist. As the first drops of blood met Chloe's tongue a fierce lust erupted inside her, and she grabbed Maggie's arm with both hands and fastened her lips to the wound, sucking on it. As the fresh blood coursed down her throat her senses began to sing and a roaring sounded in her ears. Her heart pounded as new life surged through her young body, her nipples hardened painfully and her crotch began to ache in a way it never had before. And oh, the taste!

It was an equally intense time for Maggie as well. She hadn't done this since she turned Caitlin, toward the beginning of the twentieth century. Although the sensation of blood draining from her body was worrying, the fact that she was giving her blood to feed her new 'sister' gave her a deep sense of sexual and spiritual pleasure. She leaned her head back and gasped as though experiencing an orgasm, enjoying the feeling of her life coursing out of her body to sustain Chloe. Then a sensation of warning, of panic began to sound in Maggie's brain and she knew exactly what that meant.

'That's enough!' she said sternly, yanking her arm from Chloe's grasp.

Chloe exhaled heavily and then took in a deep breath, then exhaled more slowly. She cast sheepish eyes up at Maggie and said, 'Sorry.'

'That's okay,' replied Maggie. 'If I let you drink your fill you could easily drain me and I'd probably die. You can gorge to your heart's content on a human but not on me.'

Chloe nodded understanding.

'Now wipe your mouth and chin, they're covered in blood,' said Maggie with a broad smile.

Chloe cleaned herself up under Maggie's loving gaze and then asked, 'What's it like?'

68

'What's what like?' asked Maggie.

'Giving blood to me like that.'

Maggie turned her gaze to the sky and thought for a few moments before answering. 'It's hard to describe really,' she said. 'I get a deep pleasure from doing it, physically and emotionally, it's sexually arousing and also incredibly satisfying. Although I've never experienced it myself I suppose I would liken it to a woman breastfeeding her baby.' She gave Chloe a speculative look and asked her, 'And how was your first meal?'

Chloe looked at Maggie and then a devilish glint came into her eye as she answered, 'Better than any burger.'

Maggie had to cover her mouth with both hands to prevent herself from laughing out loud. Chloe too covered her mouth as she giggled.

'Come on you!' said Maggie, aiming a mock swipe, which Chloe easily ducked. 'Let's get back.'

'Sure.'

Arm in arm the two of them walked back up the alleyway, pausing in the shadows to make sure the coast was clear before proceeding. As they walked up the road Maggie let Chloe direct them—she wanted to see what the girl would do now after feeding. The older woman was very approving when Chloe instinctively avoided the few pools of lamplight that lay between them and their destination and kept to the shadows. Chloe's instincts were sharpening, and very quickly too; to Maggie's mind that boded well for the group, very well.

They arrived back at the meeting place first and Chloe naturally gravitated towards a particularly dark spot. Maggie stood behind Chloe and wrapped her arms about the teenager's slim frame; Chloe gently grabbed Maggie's arms, snuggled into the embrace and gave a murmur of pure contentment. Maggie buried her face into Chloe's neck and murmured in kind. Chloe's gaze roved up and down the

69

street, her heightened eyesight penetrating into the deepest shadows. Despite her attention she didn't see Jen approach until she suddenly appeared out of the night ten feet away.

'Christ!' Chloe exclaimed in an almost inaudible whisper. 'Where'd she spring from?'

Jen was ten feet away but instantly heard Chloe's words and turned her head in that direction.

'There you are,' she said quietly. She looked to Maggie and asked, 'Everything go okay?'

Maggie simply nodded affirmatively and Jen nodded back in satisfaction. Then all three turned their heads towards the sound of an approaching vehicle; it was a motor home, albeit smaller than the Winnebago they had ditched earlier.

The minibus pulled up alongside where Jen, Maggie and Chloe were standing and as soon as it came to a halt Jen was walking around to the front passenger door. Maggie and Chloe followed her and climbed in the back. As soon as she entered, Chloe instantly recognised that this was a brand-new vehicle, it had that particular smell.

'Christ, Isa!' exclaimed Jen. 'Where'd you get this?'

'There's a dealership on the other side of town,' replied Isa. 'I drove this straight off the front of the lot. Then I swiped a couple of plates from a car that was at a crushing pound a bit further along. Then I had lunch.'

'It'll be nice to travel in something that hasn't had anyone else in it before,' Maggie commented.

'It'll make a nice change to drive in a vehicle with a moderately quiet engine instead of those noisy old monsters we've had of late,' said Isa. She then turned to Jen and asked, 'Dallas area?'

Jen was looking at the road map and replied, 'No, something's telling me to get north quickly.' She studied the map and then said, 'Let's head for Liberal.'

'Liberal?' enquired Isa. 'Where'n hell's that?'

'Southwest Kansas,' replied Jen, showing her friend the

70

map. 'It's the other side of the Oklahoma corridor.' The corridor Jen was referring to was a narrow strip of Oklahoma state that separated southern Kansas from northern Texas.

Isa pondered the map for a few moments and then looked out of the windshield into the night sky. 'We could get a lot further than that before daybreak,' she told Jen.

'I know,' replied Jen. 'But I don't want to go too far north until Chloe's fully up and running. We'll stay in the southern area until then.'

'Okay, Liberal it is.' And with that Isa put the van in gear and drove off.

Chapter 6

The women reached Liberal in good time even though Isa kept the vehicle within the speed limits. During the journey Jen had sat up front but hadn't really spoken, too lost in her own thoughts. Isa had tried to engage her partner a couple of times but realised that Jen just wasn't going to respond and so left her in peace. Chloe and Maggie were pretty silent too, although they sat together with arms about one another and just enjoyed being together. Finally Chloe asked, 'Who was Caitlin?'

'Someone wonderful,' replied Maggie. She then reached into a pocket on the inside of her jacket and pulled out a very battered photo. She handed it to Chloe. It was a picture of Maggie and another woman who had short, blonde hair, a slightly round face and the brightest smile you'd ever seen. Chloe noticed that the clothes Caitlin was wearing were similar to the ones she had on.

'You're a lot like she was,' said Maggie, looking at the photo with such melancholy. 'Especially in the early years, as she was only twenty when I turned her.'

'When was that?' asked Chloe.

'Ooh, let me think.' Maggie pondered a moment and then answered, 'Nineteen ten, I believe.'

'Christ!' exclaimed Chloe. 'You were together for nearly a hundred years!'

'I know,' said Maggie sadly. 'We didn't quite make it to a century together but we got close.'

Chloe could see that talking about Caitlin caused Maggie a lot of pain and so decided not to ask any more questions. However, it seemed that Maggie wanted to talk about her lost partner; there was a sad-sweet smile on her face as she continued, 'I first laid eyes on her at some society function that the three of us had gate-crashed up in Minneapolis. The moment I saw her I knew I wanted her. Her father was only a butcher but he had made such a good reputation for himself that all of the high fliers in that city patronised his shop. As a result he found himself moving in circles he otherwise wouldn't have. If he hadn't been invited to that party he wouldn't have lost his daughter.'

'Did you just nip her like you did me?' asked Chloe.

'Yeah, I did!' said Maggie with a quiet laugh. 'And I didn't even have the good manners to ask her if she wanted to come along like I did you. I just claimed her as mine.' Maggie's expression turned really sad then and she said, 'You wanna know something?'

'What?'

'She never once hated me for doing that, not once. Sure, the first four or five days she was in denial, but that was as she was turning and she never railed at me personally.' Maggie's eyes took on a faraway glint. 'She had a huge heart that girl; so much love within her. Even though I took her away from a life that she enjoyed, led her into a life of perpetual darkness, she gave me all her love without reservation. So I loved her back in kind.' She was silent a moment before adding, 'I was absolutely devastated when she was killed last year.'

'No shit,' was all Chloe could say.

Maggie remained silent after that, her mind on melancholy thoughts.

'I hope I get a love like that,' Chloe murmured to herself.

'You will, Chloe,' said Isa from the driver's seat. 'And when you do you'll wonder how you ever managed before without them.' She cast adoring eyes on Jen who was staring out the window into the night. Jen became aware of Isa's regard and laid an affectionate hand on her partner's arm. Isa's smile was painfully wonderful and Chloe was staggered at the love between the two women.

'They've been together a long, long time,' Maggie said quietly. 'My mothers.' And her gaze was adoring too.

I want to be a part of this, thought Chloe. She could be as well, but she'd have to start killing for herself, and that caused her to knot up inside.

They slipped into Liberal unnoticed and found a quiet back alley in which to park; this particular service road looked like it was hardly used. There were a couple of one-car garages but the houses behind them were dilapidated and vacant. Isa turned a questioning expression to Jen about her choice of spot. Jen got out of the van and pulled herself on top of one of the garages where she did a full survey of the area. She then climbed back down and gave Isa an affirming nod.

'All right,' she said to all of them. 'Let's stretch our legs as it's still a while 'til dawn, but don't wander too far.'

'Shall we darken this place now?' asked Maggie.

'Good idea,' replied Jen and she jumped back in the van.

Chloe was a little puzzled by the term 'darken' but that was clarified for her by what the girls did next.

Maggie delved into the large holdall and pulled out two packing-tape dispensers, two rolls of tinfoil and two rolls of masking tape. Isa pulled the strip of window tint out of her bag and handed it to Jen, then she took a tape dispenser from Maggie and laid down two strips of tape onto the windshield, about eight inches apart at eye level. She laid

74

the tape down in such a way that only one edge was stuck to the glass. Jen then took the strip of window tint and attached it to the screen with the tape Isa had put down. Isa then took a roll of tinfoil and measured some out to the width of the screen, and Jen took the tape dispenser and fastened the foil to the screen above the strip of tint; they did the same for the lower half. Then they fastened down the vertical edges with masking tape.

While Jen and Isa were working on the front windshield, Maggie took the other dispenser and ran two strips of tape top and bottom on both side windows. Chloe joined in automatically and used the tape to stick tinfoil to them; they did the same to the skylight, the rear screen and the side door's small window.

Having covered the windshield, Isa then cut away the bottom corner of foil on her side window so that she could see the side mirror clearly. She then covered this gap with some more window tint, then fastened the loose edges with masking tape. Jen did likewise on the passenger side.

The total time to complete the task was just forty seconds.

'"Darken",' said Chloe with an informed expression. 'I gotcha!'

Isa looked over her shoulder and winked at Chloe, Maggie patted her shoulder and Jen had a gentle half-smile for the teenager.

'Okay, ladies,' said Jen, 'let's get some air.'

The four of them climbed out of the vehicle and Jen wandered slowly down the alleyway, Isa close by her side. Chloe and Maggie climbed atop a nearby high wall and sat together.

'Jen's really worried, isn't she?' Chloe asked.

'Yes, she is!' said Maggie with some fervour. 'And that worries me. I've never seen her this antsy before and if Jen's unsettled then Isa and I are too.'

'Sorry about that,' Chloe apologised.

'What on earth are you apologising for?' demanded Maggie.

'Well,' began Chloe, 'none of this would be happening if I wasn't here.'

'Chloe!' admonished Maggie, putting her arms about the girl. 'This isn't your fault, it's mine! I was the one who nipped you and then was stupid enough to let you run off. I was even stupider to be seen with you earlier so don't blame yourself."

'Jen blames me though, doesn't she?'

'No she doesn't,' said Maggie firmly. 'She's annoyed with me but not with you.'

'But she's always scowling at me,' Chloe pointed out.

'She's out of sorts at the moment,' said Maggie. 'None of us has really been able to relax since Caitlin was killed, that got us real uptight. Jen's right about us getting some distance from New Mexico though—even I'm getting the feeling that we're not really safe at the moment.'

'So why didn't we travel further tonight?' asked Chloe. 'I mean, we're only just across the border in Kansas.'

'That's because you're being fed off my wrist,' replied Maggie. 'Normally we feed every other night so there's usually a fair distance between our kills. However, because I'm carrying you I have to kill every night and Jen wants to keep those kills fairly close together. Once you're feeding yourself then we'll really put some distance behind us, either New England or the north-west.'

'I don't think I'm ever gonna be able to kill for myself,' said Chloe in a sombre tone. 'It's such a horrible concept that I can hardly bring myself to even think about it, let alone do it.'

'Don't be so sure,' said Maggie with a confident smile. 'When I killed that man earlier you didn't even bat an eyelid, much less look away—I know because I was watching you. I think you'll be surprised at just how quickly you adapt to this, I think we all will actually.'

Chloe gave Maggie a grateful smile and snuggled closer to the older woman. Maggie gave a happy sigh and hugged Chloe tighter.

'Maggie?'

'Yah?'

'I'm not sorry.'

'Not sorry about what?'

'About being here with you three, about being what I am now.'

Maggie looked down at Chloe's upturned face and saw that the girl was entirely honest; Chloe Lamont was happy! There had been those few days of tantrums and tears from Caitlin at the start and Maggie could still clearly remember how angry she herself had been at first when Isa had turned her. Yet here was this girl who was just so grateful to be here, even though that meant her becoming a killer.

'Was your hometown really that bad?' she asked the girl.

'Just incredibly dull and lifeless and I'm so glad to be away from it.'

Maggie gently put her lips to Chloe's forehead and softly smooched.

'What do you want from me, Maggie?' asked Chloe. Her eyes had gone very vulnerable.

'Whatever you can freely give me,' replied Maggie. 'I've been very lonely since I lost Caitlin. I know I can't have what I had with her again as she's gone. If you can at least be my good friend, cuddle up to me when I sleep. Keep me company when those two oldsters bugger off together.' She gestured in the direction Jen and Isa had walked in. 'Just make it so that I don't feel lonely, that'd be great 'cause the last year's been pretty awful for me.'

'I like being with you already,' said Chloe. 'When I woke up this evening I was scared shitless but it was your smile that calmed me; I knew I was safe with you.'

'And you're safe with either Jen or Isa as well,' said Maggie. 'You're our new sister, never forget that.'

They sat together, side by side, with their arms about one another and just watched the night.

'Come on,' said Isa in a soft tone. 'Talk to me, old woman.'

Jen regarded Isa with such love that Isa put her arms about her partner's neck and gently forced her tongue into Jen's mouth. Jen responded in kind instantly and the two women shared the moment without thought for anything else. When they broke apart Isa looked into Jen's eyes and said, 'Talk to me, Jen, don't carry it on your own.'

'It's Chloe,' replied Jen.

'You don't like her?' Isa couldn't hide the disappointment in her voice; she adored Chloe already, considered her perfect for their group.

'Quite the opposite!' answered Jen with a startled look. 'I think she's as near perfect as you can find.'

'So what is it then?' asked Isa, eager to get to the crux of the matter so that she could ease her partner's mind.

'It's what she brings with her,' said Jen. 'We snatched her in front of witnesses, Maggie was seen with her the night before.' Jen's shoulders sagged and she said, 'That was so sloppy, what was she thinking?'

'You heard Maggie,' answered Isa. 'She wasn't thinking, she was out looking for a partner to replace Caitlin. We both know her very well; she wouldn't normally be so clumsy but in her desperation for company she slipped up.' Isa regarded Jen a moment and then continued, 'I'd be even clumsier and sloppier if I lost you.'

'Well, what's done is done and we just have to make the

best of it,' said Jen. 'But I don't feel safe, haven't felt safe really since Caitlin was killed.'

'You think that someone's after us?' asked Isa. 'And knows what we are?'

'No, I'm fairly sure that isn't the case,' said Jen with some confidence. 'After all, if someone knew about us then we'd have the full force of the FBI after us and so far I haven't seen any sign of that. But we are being pursued in the context that the police are looking for Chloe and her abductors and I'd like to get some distance from New Mexico.'

'So why'd we stop here, when we could have got further tonight?' Isa asked.

'Because Chloe's on the wrist at the moment, Mags has to kill every night and I think it's safer to keep those kills close-ish. Once Chloe's feeding herself then we can make a big leap into the northern states.'

Isa nodded understanding and then slipped her arms about Jen's neck again and put her face close. 'Just do one thing for me, would you?'

'What's that?' asked Jen.

'Go easy on Chloe, this is only her first night and she has to readjust.'

'I know,' agreed Jen. 'Although I think she's adapting far quicker than any of us did.'

'Yeah, but if you have to sound off at anyone then sound off at Mags. She's the one that put us in this situation— don't take your annoyance out on Chloe. I'm sure that Maggie will be happy to bear the full brunt of your wrath if it means Chloe's left out of it. Maggie adores that girl already.'

'I know,' said Jen with a soft smile. 'She adored Caitlin from the first moment too. She can be such a pushover.'

'Can't she!' agreed Isa with a laugh. 'Mind you, Chloe's already looking at her with doe eyes too.'

'I think that's only natural,' said Jen. 'She was abruptly uprooted from her normal life and plunged into our one; that would off-balance most people. Maggie's such a sweetie, though, that she can calm the most jittery of people.'

'That's why she's able to hunt so successfully in the way she does,' said Isa. 'Neither of us has quite her skill for drawing victims. Caitlin didn't and she was taught by Maggie.'

'Caitlin preferred group hunts,' said Jen. 'She could do it solo but far preferred having us around.'

'I wonder how Chloe'll turn out?' Isa mused.

'Probably excellently' said Jen. 'Maggie's right about her having spark, even I can see it and she hasn't calmed down properly yet. Come on, let's get back.'

And with that the two women made their way back to the van. All four of them climbed in and battened down the hatches well before dawn. Jen and Isa snuggled up together in one of the van's beds with, strangely, Jen in the submissive position. Maggie and Chloe were together in another bed.

This felt very strange to Chloe; she was getting ready to sleep but didn't feel at all sleepy. She just lay there with her head propped against Maggie's chest listening to the slow, regular heartbeat and the gentle rush of the older woman's breathing. She could feel, deep within her, the imminent appearance of the sun above the horizon and this caused her to feel uneasy, fearful even. However, when she flicked her eyes about the vehicle's interior and saw that there was no way for the sunlight to penetrate, her disquiet lessened.

Without her realising it she was suddenly deep in a dreamless sleep.

Chapter 7

That next morning Sam Morrell woke up feeling different. The reason? She wasn't alone in this any more. Louise Brody was a brand-new agent, unproven in the field, but that didn't matter to Sam; Louise *believed*. After showering, she and Brody had a light breakfast in a local diner; neither of them said anything but their eyes spoke volumes. Would they get any new leads today? After breakfast they went back into the FBI office to review what they had set in motion the day before and await any further developments. Both the e-mail inbox and the fax machine were empty and there were no messages on the answerphone so Morrell and Brody put up a map of the United States on the wall and Morrell inserted a coloured marker-pin on Fulfilment, New Mexico.

'There's our starting point,' she said to Brody. 'Let's hope that the local law enforcers are on the ball and get back to us quickly with any potential leads.'

'Will they?' Brody asked. It was a pertinent question, as she was well aware of just how little support her partner had had in the eight years she'd been on this investigation after Tacoma.

'If they don't then the body count will just keep on rising,' was Morrell's cold reply. 'These women will never stop. They can't, it's what they do, what they are. Remember this, Louise.' And her voice dropped very low so that the other agents in the office couldn't hear her. 'These women are killing but they aren't murdering, they're feeding.'

Brody gave her partner a terse nod; not murdering but feeding. In some ways that made it worse.

They spent the rest of the morning trying to figure out which way the group had gone. It was a pointless exercise and they both knew it but it occupied them, kept them focussed. Morrell was pretty sure that there would be no leads coming from the surrounding areas today. On that score she was dead wrong, because at about midday her cellphone rang.

'Special Agent Morrell,' she answered.

'Good mornin', Agent Morrell, this is Officer Melanie Daniels,' said a pleasant female voice, full of Texan twang. 'I work in the Dumas sheriff's office.'

'Good morning, Officer Daniels, how may I help you?' asked Sam.

'Well, we received an e-mail from you yesterday regardin' the abduction of a girl from New Mexico and the high probability that she had been taken by a group of women that you're pursuin',' began the Texan. 'The reason for my call is I was wonderin' how this group moved around?'

'Only at night in vehicles that they've stolen,' replied Morrell.

'What kind of vehicles?' asked Melanie.

'Usually motor homes or windowless vans although they will use anything smaller than that. No trucks though; why do you ask?'

'Well, it's probably nothin' but last night we had a vehicle reported stolen, a rather rusty Chevy Ford. Nothin' unusual in that and what's more the vehicle was found this mornin' up in Dalhart, which is about sixty miles to the northwest,' said Melanie. 'What prompted my phone call was that I went out to investigate the auto theft early this mornin' and spoke to a couple of people in that area of town. Now, one of those people owns a brand new Dodge Viper.'

'Oooh!' exclaimed Morrell mockingly. 'Is he married?'

'I rather doubt it,' said Melanie in a voice that spoke volumes. 'He really thinks he's God's gift, a plum asshole. Anyway, he's lookin' out of the window every five minutes to check that his car's still there and he saw four people lookin' at it. This was sometime in the early evenin'.'

'After sundown?' asked Morrell, all attention now.

'Yeah,' replied Daniels. 'The group moved on after about a minute and the guy thought no more of it. However, the Chevy Ford that was stolen was only a few cars down from the Dodge.'

Morrell asked Melanie, 'Was this Dodge owner able to give you any kind of description of the four people he saw?'

'Yeah,' replied Daniels. 'Although he couldn't really make too much out, he was pretty sure they were all women, one in denims, one in black leather and another in a long coat.'

Oh my God! thought Morrell. *That sounds so much like them.*

'He said that the fourth one looked to be a bit younger than the other three,' Melanie finished.

'And you say that the Chevy Ford was found in Dalhart this morning?' asked Morrell.

'Sure was,' replied Daniels.

'Have you had any murders or people reported missing last night?' Sam asked.

'No we haven't,' replied Daniels. 'Otherwise it would be the sheriff talking to you now.'

'Officer Daniels,' began Morrell, 'thank you very much for reporting this. Can I ask a huge favour of you?'

'Sure!' replied Daniels.

'I need you to check and see if there is an abandoned Winnebago either in or on the edge of your town. That was the vehicle this gang was last in,' said Morrell.

'Anythin' that would say that the Winnebago was the one they were usin'?' asked Daniels.

Morrell was impressed by this question; this police officer had the kind of mind required of a detective.

'There may be,' Sam answered. 'I know this sounds strange but this gang blocks the windows with tinfoil or plastic bags.'

'Really?'

'Yes, so if the windows are clear then look for recent signs of them having been covered—they use packing tape and that always leaves a residue behind,' finished Morrell.

'Okay, I'll get onto it right away, Agent Morrell,' Said Daniels.

'I'm going to speak to the sheriff up in Dalhart. If you find the vehicle can you call me straight away on my cellphone?' asked Sam.

'Sure thing,' said Melanie.

'Let me, or my partner, Agent Brody, know even if you don't find anything,' Sam added.

'Right, I'm gonna start lookin' now,' said Melanie. 'Oh, by the way, the sheriff up in Dalhart is Emerson Philips. A bit of a tightass but straight as an arrow. Speak to you real soon, Agent Morrell.'

'Speak to you soon, Officer Daniels.' And the connection was cut.

Sam pressed the 'end' button on her cellphone and looked up at Brody, who had an expectant expression on her face. 'We gotta lead?' She couldn't quite contain the excitement in her voice.

'Possible, very possible,' Morrell answered and went over to the map and picked up another coloured pin. 'A vehicle was reported stolen in Dumas, northwest Texas last night.' And she put the pin into the map where the town was located. 'That vehicle could easily have been stolen by kids out for a joyride, except that a witness reported seeing four

84

women in the vicinity of that vehicle who match the descriptions of our girls,' she continued. 'Now the vehicle was found this morning in Dalhart, which lies about sixty miles to the northwest of Dumas.' Another pin in the map. 'The officer I was speaking to is going to look around Dumas and see if there is a Winnebago abandoned there. If there is then it's almost certain that it's our girls.'

'Jesus,' breathed Louise. 'How fortunate can you get?'

'I'll take the leads any way they come, Louise, I've been after them a long time and I'm sick of chasing. I'm going to contact Sheriff Philips in Dalhart and speak to him. You man my cellphone just in case Officer Daniels calls back while I'm on the phone.'

Brody nodded and Sam called up Dalhart's sheriff's office on her computer. Then she picked up a phone on her desk and dialled the number displayed on her screen.

'Sheriff's office.' The person answering was a woman.

'Dalhart, northwest Texas?' Morrell verified.

'It is; how may I help you?'

'This is Special Agent Morrell of the FBI. I would like to speak with Sheriff Philips, please.' Samantha was always polite when speaking to local law enforcement. There was a long, sad history of federal and local authority not getting along. This was due, in a large part, to the Bureau officials, who affected a superior attitude and contempt when liaising with local law enforcement. Sam was of the opinion that good manners cost you nothing and could get you a long way. Sometimes this even proved to be true.

'One moment please,' said the voice on the other end and Sam heard the click as she was put on hold. There was blessed silence during the hold, no infuriating muzak. She only had to wait a few seconds before the phone was picked up again.

'Sheriff Philips speakin', how may I assist you, Agent Morrell?'

'Sheriff Philips, firstly, did you receive the e-mail from me yesterday as I didn't get around to following it up with a phone call to your office?' asked Sam.

'Yes we did, Agent Morrell,' replied Philips.

'Good, because I have very good reason to suspect that the group I am pursuing may well have passed through your jurisdiction last night,' Sam told him.

'They did?' Philips sounded alarmed.

'I'm not one hundred percent certain but I am seeking verification at this very moment,' replied Morrell. 'I was wondering, have you had any auto thefts, murders or disappearances since sundown yesterday?'

'Murders no,' replied Philips straight away. 'That I'm sure of. Auto thefts? I haven't personally dealt with any myself but I'll check with my officers. One thing I can tell you, Agent Morrell, is that we have had missin' persons reported in the last twelve hours.'

'How many?' asked Sam. Butterflies had started in her stomach.

'Three so far and what's more, none of these people had any reason to just up and leave like it appears they did, so we're treatin' these disappearances as suspect,' replied Philips.

Sam's throat went dry—Day One of this new phase in her investigation and she was getting what looked like a firm fix on them already.

'Check culverts, ditches, manholes and dumpsters,' Morrell told Philips. 'This gang hides its victims out of sight so that when the bodies do turn up a few days later the group is well away from the area.'

'I'll do just that,' Philips told her. 'You asked about stolen vehicles. I take it that's how this group gets around.'

'Yes it is,' replied Morrell. 'They'll use practically anything except trucks and big rigs but they prefer either motor homes or windowless vans.'

86

'I believe I have your contact number,' he said. 'I'll ask my officers to see if there were any vehicles reported stolen in the last twelve hours and I'll also initiate a search for any bodies. On that last one I sincerely hope you're wrong, Agent Morrell.'

'You can hope,' Sam told him. 'But I've got the feeling that this gang visited your town last night.'

'I'll make a thorough check and get back to you as soon as I have any information, or lack of it,' he told her.

'Thank you very much, Sheriff Philips,' she said. 'I greatly appreciate your assistance.'

'Not a problem,' he replied. 'At the end of the day we're all officers of the law and we're all doin' the same thing, upholdin' the law. I'll speak to you soon.' And with that he hung up.

'Good man that,' Sam said to herself as she put the phone down. She then turned to Brody and said, 'Okay, we're waiting on two phone calls, one from Dumas about the Winnebago and another one from Dalhart. Dumas is just confirmation really, it's the information that we get from Dalhart that could really put us back on their trail.'

Brody just nodded and then studied the map. Morrell joined her.

'If they did pass through Dalhart then they're heading northeasterly now,' Louise pointed out.

'Yes, they are,' Sam replied. 'They were originally heading westward until they hit Fulfilment. They've changed directions because of Chloe's abduction; they're trying to shake off any pursuit for that. I'm pretty sure they don't know that someone from the FBI's after them for the killings and I'm positive that they don't know that I'm aware of the truth about them.'

'How d'ya figure that one?' asked Brody.

'Because I'm still alive.'

Chapter 8

As soon as the sun's orange orb had descended below the horizon Jen's eyes flew open. She lay there for a couple of minutes, head resting on Isa's chest, listening to her partner's steady breathing and heartbeat. When she heard Maggie clear her throat she sat up and as soon as she had moved Isa awoke. Within twenty seconds of Maggie clearing her throat all four of them were up and instantly alert.

'What's the plan for tonight, Chief?' asked Maggie, slipping on her jeans.

Jen slipped her trousers on, then grabbed the map and studied it for a few moments before answering, 'Only you and Chloe need to feed tonight so let's get that done first and then we'll head off towards . . .' She studied the map again. 'Wichita,' she finished.

'*I am a line man for the counteeeee.*' Isa sang the first line of the Glen Campbell song. It only got her a 'babies must play' look from Jen but it did get a smile from Maggie and a small giggle from Chloe.

'Feed here?' enquired Maggie.

'*And I drive the main rooooaaad!*' Isa continued singing.

'No,' replied Jen, doing her best to ignore Isa. 'There's a small town a few miles up the road called Plains. We'll park outside of it and you two can move in, feed and quickly get out.'

'*Searchin' in the sun for another o-overload!*'

88

'ISA!'

'Oh, lighten up will ya?' Isa laughed and punched Jen on the arm. Maggie was sniggering too and Chloe nearly couldn't control her giggles.

'After you've fed we can make for Wichita.' Jen scowled at Isa, who just stuck her tongue out; then she turned to Chloe, put on her gentlest expression and said, 'Chloe, I know this is going to be hard for you but please try and make a kill yourself tonight.'

'Jen!' Maggie protested quietly. 'It's only her second night!'

'I know,' replied Jen. 'And I don't expect her to be able to, it's too soon, but I want her to at least try. So you hang back Mags, and only when Chloe fails you move in.'

Maggie reluctantly nodded.

'Let's hit the road then,' said Isa, who climbed into the driver's seat and started the van up. It purred into life and Isa smiled beatifically. 'So much better than all that clanging and banging,' she said, then put the van in gear and slowly reversed out of the service road. Twenty minutes later Isa was pulling the vehicle off the road out of sight. Maggie and Chloe got out and walked the last short distance to the town of Plains.

'Okay sweetheart,' said Maggie, 'you're gonna pick the place and the prey. I'm just going to watch and see what you do.'

'Okay,' replied Chloe, her voice shaking slightly. Although she still felt huge repugnance at the thought of killing, the prospect of 'going solo' gave her a sense of nervous excitement.

'Are you all right?' Maggie asked, a little concerned.

'Yeah,' replied Chloe. 'Just really nervous is all.'

'Well just take it easy and don't rush. I know we're in something of a hurry, but you take your time.'

They reached the town's outskirts and Maggie dropped

89

back several yards and let Chloe range ahead. She marvelled at how the younger woman instinctively kept to the shadows and stalked through the night like a tigress. After about ten minutes of walking the town's outskirts Chloe doubled back to an area she had already passed and moved into it. Maggie raised her eyebrows. Chloe had only been searching for a good killing ground and although it wasn't ideal it was nevertheless impressive for someone on their first time out. Maggie noted where Chloe was—in a narrow passageway between two buildings—and then quickly hauled herself up onto a nearby roof. How would Chloe draw a victim?

Chloe had seen how Maggie had so easily drawn a victim to her and knew there was no way she could do that and so opted for an easier way. She stayed in the shadows, unseen, and tuned herself with the night. As it was only just after nightfall there were a fair few people about but most of them were in their cars and on their way home. Two lone pedestrians did walk within range but then turned off down another road. Chloe didn't mind, she continued to wait motionless in the shadows.

Maggie was also motionless in her rooftop position and she had seen the two people come within range but then turn away. After about twenty minutes another lone pedestrian came along and Maggie could see it was a woman who appeared to be in her mid-forties. Maggie looked down and saw that Chloe had tensed up slightly. As the woman neared where Chloe was waiting the girl did something unexpected. She walked deeper into the shadows, sat down, buried her face against her knees and began to sob.

The woman heard the sobbing as she came to the passageway and stopped.

'Hello?' she called into the darkness. The only answer was continued sobbing. The woman stayed at the entrance to the passageway and peered in. After a few moments her eyes adjusted to the deep gloom and she could make out Chloe's shape most of the way down the passage.

'Are you okay?' she called. Chloe continued sobbing. The woman hesitated a moment and then entered the passageway.

On the roof Maggie was very admiring; Chloe had a natural aptitude for this as the woman had paused for less than a minute on the street before entering the passageway. Maggie had scanned up and down; no one had seen the woman. The question now was would Chloe be able to make the kill? Maggie knew that the answer was no, so she dropped to the ground behind the woman without making a sound.

'Honey, what's wrong?' the woman asked Chloe.

Finally Chloe raised her head and replied, 'You wouldn't understand.'

'Wouldn't understand what?' asked the woman in a gentle voice.

Chloe trembled all over; the woman was bent over at the waist and was in easy reach. All she had to do was strike out with her arms, grab her and sink her teeth into the woman's neck, so easy.

But she couldn't do it.

The woman saw a look of pure, unadulterated hunger come over Chloe's features and an instinctive part of her realised that she was in great danger. She straightened, backed up a couple of steps then turned to walk out of the passageway.

And ran straight in to Maggie.

Maggie struck quicker than a snake, one hand grabbed the back of the woman's head, the other clamped over the woman's mouth and her teeth sank into flesh. All within a second. As she fed, Maggie regarded Chloe, who was staring at the grisly scene before her, not flinching.

Good girl, thought Maggie.

Having gorged on the woman's blood Maggie let the corpse slump to the floor and emitted a wet belch. She swayed a little and quietly said, 'Woo, what a rush.'

Chloe got up and said, 'I couldn't quite bring myself to do it.' Her face and voice betrayed her disappointment.

'I know,' replied Maggie, wiping her mouth and chin. 'But you came real close. You're a natural at this, you found a pretty good spot and I have to say that the sobbing was a good trick to draw her in. I'm impressed.'

'She's probably a mother so the sound of a youngster crying would draw her,' explained Chloe sombrely.

'Don't even think about it, Chloe,' said Maggie quietly, cupping the girl's chin. 'Remember, we're the lions.'

Chloe nodded then bent down and picked the woman up, putting the corpse over her right shoulder. Chloe was surprised at just how light the woman was. Then she thought about it again; the woman looked to be about thirty pounds overweight. The woman wasn't light; it was she who was now really strong. Chloe turned around and walked down the passageway to the rear of the buildings where there were some low-lying bushes. Chloe scanned the terrain in front of her and saw that there was a ditch running behind the bushes. She walked over to it and saw that it was fairly deep. Chloe dropped the body to the ground and relieved the woman of her cash, not much, only thirty dollars and no credit cards, which she stuffed into her jacket pocket. She then held out her hand to Maggie. She heard a metallic *click-click-click* and felt the butterfly knife placed in her hand. Chloe took a deep breath and then deliberately ran the keen blade across the woman's throat, slitting it all the way and obliterating Maggie's bite mark. She wiped the blade on the woman's clothes and then handed the knife back to Maggie; *click-click-click* as it was

92

sheathed. Chloe pushed the woman's body into the ditch and then regarded it; still a bit too visible. So she walked over to a small bush nearby, grabbed its main stem near the ground and heaved. The bush came up easily and Chloe put the bush on top of the woman's body, completely covering it. She then looked at Maggie.

'Is this okay?' she asked.

'Sure is!' replied Maggie. 'They won't find her for at least a couple of days, I suspect. Come on, let's get back to the others. I can feed you in the van.'

Chloe nodded and the two of them made their way back to where Isa had parked the van, Maggie once again letting Chloe lead and once again approving of the way the girl kept to the shadows. Unseen.

Back at the van Jen asked Maggie, 'How'd it go?'

'Very well really,' replied Maggie. 'She couldn't make the kill herself but everything else went like clockwork.'

'Good,' said Jen. She then turned a smile to Chloe and said, 'Try again tomorrow night?'

'Sure thing, Jen,' replied Chloe, who dug her hand into her pocket and pulled out the thirty dollars in crumpled bills. 'This was all she had on her,' she added, offering the money to Jen.

Jen smiled approvingly and replied, 'You keep it, we've all got enough.'

Isa put the van in gear and drove on down the highway, heading for Wichita. Chloe surprised her three companions when Maggie was feeding her. Just before Maggie was about to yank her wrist free with the words, 'That's enough,' Chloe voluntarily raised her head from the wound and wiped her mouth.

'You know when to stop?' Maggie exclaimed; her look was incredulous.

'You gotta be shittin' me!' Isa said from the driver's seat.

Chloe shrugged her shoulders. 'I just sensed that I was bringing you down to the danger level and so stopped drinking,' she told Maggie.

'I'm so stunned that you *voluntarily* stopped drinking,' Maggie said in a quiet voice. 'I remember the bitch of a time I used to have getting Caitlin off my wrist.'

'I remember the bitch of a time I had getting you off my wrist!' Isa told Maggie and all three women burst out laughing.

Chloe smiled at the banter—she wanted to be part of it; she wanted to *become*.

The road they were travelling on was fairly busy with traffic and that suited Jen just fine; while the other two had been out feeding she and Isa had taken down the tinfoil so that their vehicle wouldn't be too conspicuous. They reached Wichita with no trouble and quickly set about finding a good spot to bed down for the day. Once that had been found it only took forty seconds to darken the vehicle again and then they went out into the night and stretched their legs.

'Are we feeding here tomorrow night?' Maggie asked Jen.

'Sure are!' replied Jen. 'This is a big place, big enough to hide two or even three lots of kills and not have them discovered for some time.'

'Where are we headed afterward?' asked Isa.

'If Chloe can make a kill herself then we'll go north and head in to Minnesota,' replied Jen. 'If she can't then I think it might be wise to jink southeast into Oklahoma. While she's on the wrist I want to stay down here but we have to keep moving.'

'We've got plenty of room down here in the south,' said Maggie. 'I can understand your reasons for wanting Chloe feeding herself as soon as, but why push it?'

'Because I'm worried,' replied Jen. 'Anyway, we'll see what tonight brings us and then decide on how to proceed.'

Jen and Isa suddenly walked away then and Chloe wondered what was up until she saw Maggie's gentle smile.

'A bit of quality time before we bed down for the day?' Chloe asked quietly.

Maggie just nodded, still wearing the smile. Chloe sat there awkwardly with her hands in her lap. She was incredibly attracted to Maggie but didn't know how to communicate it. They sat there in silence, occasionally making eye contact, and when they did look at each other Chloe would blush and Maggie would turn shy. Eventually Chloe went and sat next to Maggie and leaned against her. Maggie responded with a comforting arm about her shoulders. They remained like that until Jen and Isa returned.

All four of them climbed into the van well before dawn, shucked off their jackets, trousers and shoes and climbed into bed. Once again Chloe was struck by how strange it felt, to lie there ready for sleep and yet feel unsleepy. She lay there with her head on Maggie's chest and, as with the morning before, her unease rose with the imminent arrival of sunrise. She raised herself up slightly and looked down into Maggie's adoring eyes.

'See you this evening,' said Chloe and gently kissed Maggie.

'I'll be waiting,' replied Maggie after catching her breath; Chloe's kiss had caught her completely by surprise.

Chloe laid her head back on Maggie's chest and, as with the morning before, one moment she was wide awake and the next moment there was darkness.

As Chloe was falling asleep Sam was driving into Oklahoma City. Louise was fast asleep in the passenger seat; she had driven the first half of the journey up from Albuquerque, during which time Sam had used the opportunity to catch some zees herself. Sam had made the decision to base herself in Oklahoma after Melanie Daniels and Sheriff Philips had called her back. Daniels reported that she had found an abandoned Winnebago on the outskirts of Dumas—the windshield was clear but there was tape residue on it and the other windows were still covered.

A couple of hours later Sheriff Philips of Dalhart reported that two of his missing persons had been found murdered in the town and that a motor-home dealership had reported one of its new vehicles stolen, a Roadtrek Versatile. Being brand new, the vehicle had no licence plates but it wouldn't be too much trouble to swipe plates from another vehicle. Philips was checking to see if any car in town had had its plates stolen; so far there had been nothing. He added that both murder victims had had their throats slit; Sam didn't tell him that the cuts were only there to hide the bite marks. Most of the victims attributed to the group usually had their throats slit although she was sure the group had other ways of hiding their feeding. Sam was also sure that even she wasn't fully aware of just how many people these women had killed over the years. When she first took on the case she was only looking for multiple murders, of which there were quite a few, but when she discovered that they were actually feeding off their victims she realised that the death toll would be astronomically higher than she had calculated. Sometimes they would hunt as a group but she figured that most of the time they fed solitarily from one another; single killings didn't stick out so much.

With Daniels and Philips confirming that the group had passed through their towns, Sam and Louise had studied the map. The group was heading in a northeasterly direction and in short hops, but she knew what these girls were like; they could really move when they wanted to and being in the centre of the country gave them the options of both east and west.

Sam wondered if the shortness of their journeying so far was to give Chloe time to fully become one of them; it seemed likely. Once Chloe was feeding like them then Sam was sure that they would move far greater distances between stops, and that was why she had decided to head northward herself.

If she could only get in front of them, lie in wait for them, have them come to her.

But that was just wishful thinking; apart from Tacoma and Scottsbluff, Sam had always been following in their wake. Nevertheless, she was going to try and get ahead of them and maybe, just maybe, she might have a chance of catching them when it was daylight. She had, after all, done it once before.

She pulled up outside the Bureau offices just as the sun was clearing the horizon. When she switched the engine off Brody slowly woke up with a groan and a lazy, lethargic stretch.

'Rise and shine!' Sam said in a bright and cheerful voice.

'What time is it?' Brody mumbled.

'Just after five-thirty in the morning,' Sam replied cheerily.

'Jesus!' Louise muttered. 'Didn't you know that it's positively forbidden to chirp at this time of the morning?'

Sam laughed and said, 'Guess what? I don't care!'

Brody laughed and straightened up in her seat. 'What now?' she asked.

'Put all law enforcement in this neck of the woods on alert,' replied Sam. 'The girls are in the area and we need to hammer that home to the locals. Every disappearance needs to be investigated and quickly, and searches made of the nearby area to see if there have been any kills. It is possible to track these girls but we need to be on our toes at all times.'

'We need more agents on this one,' Brody pointed out.

'You don't have to tell me,' replied Sam. 'But I think it's too soon. Once we get some definite sightings of them though, well, I'm gonna light such a huge fire under the Bureau's ass they ain't gonna know what's hit them.'

'The gloves gonna come off then?' asked Brody with a smile.

'You betcha!' said Morrell with some heat. 'The Bureau owes me for the last eight years. If it weren't for me then nobody would have a clue about these killings.'

Sam then regarded her partner with very soft eyes and it struck Louise at that moment just how tired Samantha Morrell was. She'd been carrying this on her own for eight years, six knowing what she was after; one person could only do so much and Sam looked close to the end at that moment. Louise reached out and gently gripped Sam's arm.

'Hey partner,' she said in a soft voice. 'I'm here as well. Just a little longer and we can see an end to this case.'

Morrell's cast-iron mask slipped a little then and Brody caught a glimpse of something that probably nobody else in the Bureau had ever seen, the hurt little girl that lay behind the agent.

'I hope you're right, Louise,' Sam said quietly. 'Because if they go off the radar again then I won't be able to stick it out for when they return. These girls have got plenty of something that I don't have. Time.'

Brody nodded and then said, 'Before we get started there is one important thing we have to do first.'

'What's that?' asked Morrell.

'Get some breakfast, I'm starving!'

Sam's laughter was agreement enough.

Chapter 9

Colorado, Kansas, Missouri and Kentucky. Nebraska, Iowa and Illinois. After breakfast Morrell and Brody had been on the phone constantly to local police in all those states, alerting them that a group of wanted killers may be coming their way. As before, some took the calls seriously, some not so seriously. By two-thirty that afternoon Sam was exhausted; she could see that Brody was too and decided to call it a day and head for bed as a couple of hours' sleep in a car wasn't really rest.

Just before she left the office, Morrell's cellphone rang.

'Special Agent Morrell,' she answered.

'Sam? It's Jim Wagner from New Mexico.'

'Hi there, Jim,' replied Sam. 'What's up?'

'Just a couple of things from Earl Bergman,' began Wagner. 'Firstly a group of teenagers saw Chloe Lamont the night before she was abducted in the diner. She was in the company of a woman who was from out of town.'

'I've already got that info, Jim,' replied Sam. 'But it's nice to have it fully confirmed.'

'I thought you would have,' said Wagner. 'That's just Earl Bergman trying to be a sheriff. Second bit of news is that Rachael Lamont has disappeared.'

Morrell's stomach plunged downwards. 'How?' she asked.

'Seems she took off in the middle of the night,' replied Wagner. 'Took her mother's car and vanished. Ruth

Lamont reckons that Rachael has gone to look for Chloe as they were very close. I guess they were, being twins.'

'How on earth does Rachael expect to find Chloe?' Sam was only asking the question to herself but she had asked it out loud.

'I don't know,' Jim answered. 'But they are twins, so maybe Rachael can home in on her sister in some way.'

'I hope for her sake that she can't!' exclaimed Morrell. 'Chloe is in with some *very* nasty company. If Rachael does get close it could easily be the death of her.'

'Well, I've alerted Texas and Oklahoma states to be on the lookout for her but I thought I'd let you know.'

'Thanks for doing that, Jim,' said Morrell and she was genuinely grateful. 'Once this is over I'll drop by and buy you a beer or ten.'

'I'm looking forward to it already,' Wagner laughed. 'Any more news and I'll pass it on.'

'Thanks Jim, speak to you later.'

' 'Bye Sam, you take care.'

Sam ended the call and then said, 'Shit! I don't need this!'

'What's up?' asked Brody.

'Chloe's twin sister Rachael has left home and is probably searching for her.'

'Needle in a haystack sound familiar?' queried Brody with raised eyebrows.

'I hope so,' said Sam with a troubled expression. 'I don't need a loving sister jumping into the middle of this and screwing things up.'

'I don't think there's any chance of that,' said Brody. 'She doesn't know where to start looking so she'll probably flounder around New Mexico and Texas.'

'The problem there,' began Sam with a serious expression, 'is that our girls passed through northern Texas and Rachael might stumble across that info.'

'The chances of Rachael discovering that are a million to one though,' Brody pointed out.

'Anyway,' said Sam, waving her hand dismissively. She wasn't going to let Rachael Lamont worry her just yet. 'Let's get some sleep.'

'We'll be waking up sometime this evening if we get our heads down now,' protested Brody.

'I know,' replied Sam. 'I think we need to become part night owl if we're to have any chance of catching up with them.'

'And you've been doing this for six years?'

'Six knowing what I was chasing, but this is my tenth year in total on this case.'

Brody gave a low whistle.

'Come on, shut-eye time.' It was almost an order. Brody answered it with a huge yawn.

Rachael Lamont felt incredibly guilty but what else was she to do? While Chloe was sleeping the day away in the back of a Winnebago in Tucumcari, Rachael and her mother had wandered around the house like shell-shock victims. Chloe's abduction had left Ruth Lamont distraught and tearful but it had absolutely devastated Rachael. That was the problem when you were a twin, your sibling was more than just a sibling, she was the other half of you. With Chloe taken away Rachael's only feeling was that of a hollow shell. Once night had fallen Chloe's absence was even more pointed—the house didn't echo to the sound of the FM rock station that Chloe always listened to. There wasn't the sound of heated voices as Chloe and Momma argued yet again. There was so much about this house that spoke of Chloe, but with no Chloe present that only amplified the loss Rachael felt. She had gone to bed early but took a long time getting off to sleep, as she kept going over and over the conversation she'd had with the FBI agent that morning. She was certain of one thing: Agent Morrell knew a lot more about what had happened to Chloe than she'd let on. And what about when she had described the Winnebago's windshield? The look in Morrell's eyes! Triumph mixed with fear. Rachael was certain that her sister was in serious trouble.

When she awoke it was still dark outside; a look at the clock told her that it was only two-thirty in the morning. She tried rolling over and getting back to sleep but she wasn't able to and spent the rest of the night tossing and turning. When she got up next morning she was grainy-eyed and totally out of sorts. The rest of the day was spent either napping or wandering around like a zombie. Rachael preferred it when she was asleep; she couldn't feel Chloe's loss then.

She woke again in the early hours of next morning; she had felt something within her and instantly realised that it was Chloe. Despite the abduction and all the worry that had caused, Rachael was convinced that her sister was still alive. If Chloe were dead then Rachael would have felt it. Rachael knew that Chloe was out there and moving around, and it was in that moment that she decided to go and find her sister.

After dressing, a quick check showed that her mother was fast asleep. She left her an apologetic note, emptied her cash box that she kept in the bedside cabinet and was surprised to find a rather large amount of money in it. She had obviously forgotten to deposit most of it into her bank-account. She grabbed her bank account book and her mother's car keys and quietly crept out into the darkness. She half expected lights to come on in the house when she started the car up but there was nothing; Momma was obviously deeply asleep. Then she headed off into the night, but where to go? She had no idea, but she could *feel* that her twin was north and east somewhere and so, trusting her instincts, she headed out of Fulfilment and onto the open road. Although she had lived here all her life she had only ever gone as far as Tucumcari and the thought of venturing so far, on her own too, gave her a thrill. But the thrill did nothing to compensate for the aching emptiness within her, that could only be filled by Chloe's return.

She half expected to be pulled over by a cop and that would be the end of her quest as she didn't have any insurance or even a driver's licence. However, no one stopped her and she carried on through the night. She stopped at a roadside diner around six that morning in Buffalo, northern Oklahoma and had herself some breakfast. The diner was empty save two truckers sitting in separate booths. Rachael chose herself a booth and quaked inwardly when the waitress came to take her order. She was relieved when the waitress just took her order and then went away again; no awkward questions were asked and no one remarked on her presence.

As she sat there eating her breakfast she could feel that her sister was out there and Rachael wondered how Chloe was. Was she scared? Was she hurt? Rachael didn't know and it was the not knowing that hurt, that drove her to try and find Chloe. After breakfast she filled up at a gas station and headed out once more. She had no destination in mind as she was only following her gut instinct.

No one truly understands the bond between twins, what sharing a womb for nine months does to the babies, but everyone agrees that there is an inexplicable link between the siblings. And that link was proving true, for early that afternoon Rachael finally pulled up at a motel; she needed to sleep although she was anxious to follow Chloe.

The motel was on the outskirts of Wichita.

*

The sun had dropped below the horizon and Jen's eyes immediately flew open. She took in a deep breath and then exhaled slowly. As she stretched she heard Isa draw in a large breath and knew that her partner had awoken—they always woke within moments of each other. Across the van she heard Maggie clear her throat and Chloe give a low groan; they were all awake. Jen lay there with her head on Isa's chest, just revelling in the moment. Across the van she could hear the quiet murmurs of Maggie and Chloe, fully entering the first stages of falling in love with each other. It made her smile and remember when she had first met Isa all those many, many years ago.

'Okay girls,' she said once they were all sitting up. 'We're in Wichita but I don't want to spend too long here so let's be on our way in, say, two hours?'

Isa, Maggie and Chloe nodded agreement.

'Any plans as to where we go from here?' asked Maggie.

'That all depends on whether Chloe can feed herself tonight or not,' replied Jen. 'If she can, then I reckon a long haul up into Minnesota. If not, then maybe head east and south into Oklahoma. Let's play it by ear, shall we?'

Nods all round and then they were taking down the tinfoil and getting ready to go out into the night.

Rachael had arrived in Wichita at about two o'clock that afternoon; she slept until just after seven, when she suddenly snapped awake. Chloe was close by, she could feel it. She rose and quickly showered then checked out. She was a bundle of nervous energy; Chloe was here, she *knew* it. She drove into one area of the city and instantly realised that she was going the wrong way. She did an illegal U-turn in the road, eliciting angry honks from other car drivers, and headed back a ways before entering another district. This time she was almost jigging in her seat; Chloe was close, oh she was so *close*! Rachael parked the car up and walked the streets, eyes scanning everybody she saw. She was unaware of the strange looks she was getting from passers-by and wouldn't have cared if she was aware; her only intent was to find her sister. She kept looking.

By nine o'clock that night Morrell and Brody were awake once more; a few hours' sleep in a proper bed followed by a nice, hot shower had revived them and they were fully alert. They studied the map.

'Where do you think they are?' Louise asked Sam.

'My guess is somewhere north of here,' replied Morrell. 'I still need to follow in their wake at the moment, make sure I'm still behind them before I try and jump ahead. Besides, it was a long enough journey from Albuquerque to here.'

Brody nodded and asked, 'Why here and not, say, Denver?'

'There's every possibility that they could suddenly head west even though they're heading easterly at the moment,' replied Morrell. 'However, human settlements get further apart to the west whereas they get closer together if you go east. I figure that they'll continue northeasterly for a couple of nights and mingle with the denser population found there. I'm thinking that they're still trying to evade pursuit over Chloe's abduction so I don't want to get too close for the moment. However, I don't want to get too far behind either.'

'It's a tricky one this,' commented Brody.

'You don't have to tell me!' said Morrell. 'But if we happen to discover where they're sleeping the day away then we'll have to act really fast in order to capitalise on the daylight. That's the only time they're vulnerable. But we will still have to be extremely careful; when I killed Caitlin

Baker last year four police officers died. These women are very dangerous even when it's daytime and they've only just woken up.'

'We'll get them, Sam,' said Brody with quiet conviction. 'We're onto them now and they won't get away.'

'They won't if we don't spook them,' said Morrell. Just then her cellphone rang and she answered it.

'Agent Morrell, this is Emerson Philips here in Dalhart, Texas. A little update for you about the stolen Roadtrek.'

'Go ahead, Sheriff Philips,' said Sam.

'Nothin' much to report really, only that no car owners here have reported havin' their licence plates stolen.'

'They wouldn't drive around in an unplated vehicle,' Sam stated.

'Well, they wouldn't have to,' said Emerson. 'A short distance from the dealership is an auto pound so they could have obtained some plates from there.'

'Texas plates only?' asked Sam hopefully.

'If only life could be that simple.' Philips laughed ruefully. 'We're in the northwest corner of the state here so we get vehicles with plates from all over. Mostly New Mexico, Oklahoma and Kansas with a little bit of Colorado. Obviously there'll be the odd car in the pound from a lot further away too.'

'It was too much to hope for,' said Sam. 'But thank you anyway for your efforts on this case, I greatly appreciate it.'

'No problem, Agent Morrell,' replied Philips. 'As I said before, we're both doin' the same job of upholdin' the law. Only your jurisdiction is far, far bigger than mine and I don't envy you it.'

Sam laughed and said, 'Thank you very much, Sheriff Philips. Maybe we'll speak again at some point.'

'Very well, Agent Morrell, glad to be of some help to you. Goodbye.'

Sam ended the call and looked to Brody.

'Good or bad news?' Louise asked.

'The vehicle they're in could have Texas, New Mexico, Oklahoma or Kansas plates,' replied Sam.

'That narrows it down a bit then, doesn't it?' said Brody with a tight grin.

'Then again, it could have plates from any of the forty-nine states on the mainland.' And Morrell shrugged her shoulders.

Chapter 10

'Listen up, Chloe,' said Maggie as the four of them were walking down a well-lit street. 'It's a bit different tonight as we're in a major population centre and it's still fairly early.' She kept her voice low so as not to be overheard by any passers-by. 'Although there are a lot of people around, which means we can blend in easier, it also means more potential witnesses should we be careless.'

'Add to that that the police are looking for you, Chloe,' said Jen back over her shoulder. 'I don't know if they're looking for you this far upcountry, but play it safe.'

'Sure thing,' Chloe replied. She resolved to make a kill on her own, tonight even, although she still felt sick thinking about it.

'Yeah, so we have to be even more selective about where and who we . . . take,' said Maggie.

'Hunt together?' asked Chloe quietly.

'Let's find a good spot first, that'll determine how we go about it,' was Maggie's reply.

They reached a main street and Jen turned to Maggie and Chloe and said, 'Okay girls, we'll split up here. See you back at the van in two hours.'

'Happy huntin',' said Maggie, giving her two sisters a cheery salute.

'You too, youngsters,' Isa shot back, and with that she and Jen crossed the road.

Chloe and Maggie toured the streets for about half an hour. Chloe had seen a couple of sites that looked good to her but Maggie had shaken her head. Too open, too busy, she had said. Chloe regarded the areas again, trying to see what faults Maggie had found, and she thought that she could. Finally Chloe saw a spot and looked to Maggie, who regarded it a moment before nodding.

It was a service road that served two rows of workshops and garages; there was a dumpster beside every door. The service road ended in a high brick wall topped with barbed wire that was hanging down in a couple of places. On the wall was a single, dim lamp that only created a small pool of light; the rest of the service road lay in total darkness. Chloe and Maggie stood in the shadows just inside the entrance to the road and there they waited. Ten minutes later a group of five pedestrians, laughing and chatting, walked straight past where the two hunters were standing without seeing them. It was only the fact that there were five people that saved them. Ten minutes after that two young men came walking down the road and Chloe immediately focussed on the night. There wasn't anybody else nearby; these two were viable targets. Chloe was desperate to make a kill; if she could feed herself then it would allow the group greater freedom of movement, and so without consulting Maggie she stepped briefly into the light and then back into shadow. It was a clumsier copy of the move she had seen Maggie make two nights ago but it had the desired effect; she had drawn the eye of both men. She moved slowly and deliberately in the lighter shadows to let them know that someone was there and once she was sure she had their undivided attention she allowed her face to partially enter the light. Just as with Maggie two nights previously, the men crossed the street towards her in order to get a closer look. Chloe slowly walked into the service road and as soon as she was out of their line of sight she sprinted the full length of the road so that she was by the brick wall, half in and half out of the dim pool of lamplight. She leaned nonchalantly against the wall and waited for the men to come to her.

Maggie was caught off guard when Chloe stepped in and out of the light. A quick check told her that the coast was clear and that the two men approaching were alone. She realised almost straight away what Chloe was doing, she was leaving herself with no choice but to make a kill. That could be dangerous; Maggie was of the opinion that Chloe wasn't ready to kill yet, which could mean that one, or both, of these men could get away when Chloe faltered. So Maggie kept motionless in the shadows and the two men had no idea she was there even though they passed within five feet of her. She watched as they advanced to where Chloe was standing, and she saw them affect swaggers and alter their body posture in an attempt to look cool and alluring to females.

Chloe stood leaning against the brick wall, staring at the ground. She was very tense and it took her some moments to get her heart to stop racing; she needed to be very cool and controlled in this situation. She looked up without raising her head and saw the two men swaggering towards her. Behind them she could see Maggie stalking through the shadows.

'Hey there darlin'!' called out one of the men. 'What you doin' all by your lonesome?'

'Trying to be alone,' replied Chloe in a sullen tone. She folded her arms across her chest in a display of petulance.

'Why would a pretty thing like you want to be alone?' asked the other man.

'Because the people I came here with are really pissing me off,' replied Chloe in a 'spoilt brat' voice.

'Being on your own is not the best cure for that,' said the first man.

110

'And what is?' asked Chloe in a quiet voice. She raised her head and made eye contact with him.

'Why, being in better company!' replied the man with a broad smile as he spread his arms wide.

'Sure!' said the other. 'Why don't you come along with us and we'll show you a good time.'

'Really?' Chloe smiled at the two men and their faces brightened even more.

'Yeah, we know lots of good places around here,' said the first man.

Chloe cast her eyes downwards and gave them a shy smile, which caused the two men to automatically step closer to her. Behind them she could see Maggie creeping forward, as silent as a ghost.

'Where would we go to first?' She focussed on one of the men.

'I know a great place,' he replied. 'Cold beer, hot live bands every night and a great atmosphere.' He was gesturing as he said this and Chloe knew that she had hooked him; Maggie knew it too because she circled behind them to close in on the other man.

Maggie got into position but she could see from Chloe's posture that the girl would not be able to make the final move and actually sink her teeth in. Nevertheless, she was impressed by the way Chloe was playing this, calm and composed on the inside but coquettish and very appealing on the outside. She saw Chloe tense up, ready to strike and so readied herself.

Chloe wound herself up to make the final move; she could practically hear the man's blood pumping through his veins and her bloodlust rose. She made a final check and saw that Maggie was in position behind the other guy. Now was the time but as she stepped towards 'her' man, reluctance suddenly rose up within her and she began to lose some of her composure.

111

'Where would we go after that?' she asked, her voice faltering, and she trembled ever so slightly.

'Where would you like to go?' asked the man. 'I know plenty of places to go to after hours.'

Maggie winced—that had to be one of the *worst* come-on lines she'd ever heard.

'Oh, I don't know,' replied Chloe, who was now desperately trying to figure out a way to make the kill; biting into his neck was just too repulsive. 'How about somewhere intimate?'

'We know lots of places like that,' said the second man and Chloe could hear the leer in his voice.

Inspiration came to Chloe then and she simply said into the shadows, 'Grab him!' Then she straight-arm punched 'her' man in the face. Chloe didn't hit him that hard but his feet left the floor as he sailed back four feet before hitting the ground.

Maggie had seen Chloe wind herself up for the final move and had seen the girl begin to falter. Maggie's heart had gone out to Chloe; she was trying *so* hard, but now was the danger time. These guys would sense something wrong in a moment and would run for it. She had been wondering how to finish this quickly and cleanly when Chloe had said 'grab him' to her. She had then watched as Chloe punched 'her' guy off his feet and then turned on the other man.

The other guy watched in amazement as this young girl sent his friend literally flying. He turned to see her stepping towards him and instinctively backed up, only to find himself suddenly grabbed in a vice-like grip, a hand clamped over his mouth. He tried to struggle but whoever had hold of him was immensely strong. He was bent over backwards slightly, which immobilised him even more.

'What are you doing?' Maggie asked, looking up from her captive.

'Improvising,' replied Chloe, who was looking at the man

112

she had punched. 'He's out for the count,' she murmured, then turned to Maggie and said, 'I couldn't bring myself to bite but I have an idea.' She then reached into Maggie's jacket pocket and pulled out the butterfly knife. She opened it up and then said to Maggie, 'Hold him steady.'

'I've got him,' replied Maggie, who couldn't quite believe what she thought Chloe was about to do.

Chloe held the knife firmly in her right hand and stepped up to the man who was now desperately struggling to get away. His eyes widened in terror when he saw the knife coming towards him. Chloe took a deep breath and then sliced into the man's neck, severing his jugular vein. She wasn't expecting the blood to come out quite *that* fast as it jetted into her face, and she instinctively flinched back. Then the predator inside her took over and as quick as lightning she fastened her mouth to the fountain's source, drinking deeply.

'Take all that you want,' Maggie said quietly. 'Drink your fill.' She was absolutely stunned that Chloe had made a kill and on only her third night! Caitlin had taken four weeks and Maggie herself had taken four months to do that. 'Well done Chloe, well done,' she murmured, her voice glowing with pride.

To Chloe nothing had ever tasted this sweet. She had already fed twice but there was something extra special about taking it in this way; she could feel it as she drank, her body coming alive even more than when she had fed from Maggie's wrist. By the time she released her mouth from the wound the man was dead; Chloe belched quietly and then straightened up. And then fell flat on her arse.

'Woo!' she said quietly, putting her hand to her head. 'I'm spinnin'.'

'Quite a kick, ain't it?' said Maggie, letting the body fall to the floor. 'After a short while you'll get used to taking that much and won't feel so knocked out.'

113

After about a minute Chloe got to her feet and wiped her mouth clean. Maggie walked over to where the other man was still lying, unconscious. As Maggie fed, Chloe pondered on how best to hide these kills. The most obvious place to dump the bodies was in one, or two, of the dumpsters. How to hide Maggie's bite though? Just slitting the throat like before might give some sharp-eyed detective a clue. Chloe's eyes were drawn to the wall and an idea came to her. She collapsed the butterfly knife and walked over to where some of the barbed wire was hanging down. By bending a loose end back and forth a few times she was able to snap off a length of wire about foot or so long, and then she snapped off another similar length of wire. As she walked back Maggie was standing up and wiping her mouth.

'Have you got my knife?' Maggie asked.

'Yeah, but we're not using it on these guys,' replied Chloe. 'We've done that two nights running so I think we should do something different tonight.' And she handed Maggie a length of barbed wire. Maggie looked at it with some confusion until she saw what Chloe was doing.

After dragging 'her' corpse out of the lamplight and into the shadows, Chloe stuck a barb into the slit she had drunk from, then she wrapped the rest of the wire around the man's neck a couple of times, twisting the ends to make it look like he had been garrotted. She then dragged the body over to one of the dumpsters in which she found some strips of nylon binding, the kind used to keep cardboard cartons from splitting open. She used the binding to tie the man's hands and feet before depositing him in the dumpster, and then rearranged some of the detritus within to conceal the body from casual inspection. When she turned around she saw Maggie was doing the same.

The two of them slipped quietly out of the service road, keeping to the shadows until they were some distance away.

Then they relaxed and walked at a normal pace, two women out for an evening stroll.

'Well done, Chloe,' Maggie said quietly, hardly able to contain the delight in her voice. 'You've made your first kill.'

'Technically it wasn't a kill,' Chloe murmured back. 'I couldn't actually bite.'

'Doesn't matter.' Maggie said with a quiet laugh. 'What's important is that you won't have to feed tomorrow night, which means we can really put some miles behind us.'

They fell silent as they were now on a busy street and there was a young man walking towards them. As they entered a pool of lamplight his features brightened and he said, 'Evening ladies!'

'Good evening!' the girls chorused at him with bright smiles as they walked past. Chloe looked back over her shoulder and saw that the man was still walking forward but was looking backwards at them.

'Watch that lamppost!' she cried out to him.

He suddenly stopped mid-stride and swung his head around, but there was no lamppost.

'Gotcha that time!' Chloe called out to him as she carried on down the street with Maggie laughing along.

The man shook his head wryly at having been duped, then carried on his way.

They reached the van and saw that Jen and Isa were already there waiting. Jen looked like she was about to ask Maggie something but stopped when she laid eyes on Chloe.

'She has.' Jen was unsure. 'Hasn't?'

'Technically no,' Maggie answered. 'But she has drunk her fill so we've got tomorrow night off.'

Jen looked confused by this and so Maggie added, 'She couldn't bite him so she used my knife to open his vein and then drank from it.'

Jen's face erupted with a delighted expression. 'Oh Chloe!' And she swept the teenager off her feet in a massive hug and kissed her soundly on the mouth.

'Steady Jen!' Chloe laughed after they broke apart. 'You'll make Mags and Isa jealous.'

'Bah! They'll just have to live with it.' Jen looked like she was about to shed a tear or two she looked so happy.

'She's definitely one of us now,' said Isa, her eyes glowing as she enveloped Chloe in an equally massive hug and kissed her soundly. After that Chloe was ready to shed a tear.

'Come on,' said Jen. 'Let's get out of here.' They all climbed into the van and Jen looked at the map. 'Isa, do you think we can get to Omaha, Nebraska before sunrise?'

Isa looked at the map for a few moments then looked out the windshield. 'Should do it,' she replied. 'Dawn's still a way off so yeah, we'll get there before daybreak and maybe even find somewhere to park up too.'

'That settles it then, Omaha it is.' She folded the map and then asked Jen, 'Do you want me to drive tonight?'

'That's okay, Grandma,' replied Isa grandly, patting Jen's knee. 'I'll drive and you can rest your old bones.'

Jen didn't bother replying to that, she just punched Isa's arm. Hard.

Rachael was in constant motion now. She knew, just *knew* that Chloe was close. She was now stalking the streets like a tigress, her eyes scanning everywhere. People were giving her a wide berth because she looked positively dangerous, so intent was she on finding Chloe. She saw a man walking towards her and he had a quizzical expression on his face, a finger ready to point at her. Realisation dawned on her really quickly.

'You've seen me before?' she demanded.

'Yeah, about five minutes ago,' replied the man.

Rachael's excitement went through the roof. 'Where?'

'Just down the road,' he said, pointing back the way he came. 'You were with a dark-haired woman.'

'That wasn't me!' she shouted to him as she sprinted in the direction he indicated.

For the second time that night the man shook his head wryly.

Rachael pounded down the pavement, her head swinging from side to side, scanning every person she could see. She checked down side streets and if there were people in them then she would get closer to check them. After about twenty minutes she was winded and swearing profusely; she had criss-crossed the whole of this part of town but could not find Chloe. She had accosted passers-by and shown them a photo of her sister; described the clothes she was wearing, brown leather jacket, dark blue jeans and white sneakers. No one she asked had seen her. She had come so close! It made her want to cry but she refused tears and she refused to give up.

Come on Rachael, think!

She could sense roughly which direction Chloe was in but that was about it, it was just sheer good fortune that someone who had seen Chloe had seen her a few minutes later. She needed a better way to locate her sister. As she walked back to where her car was parked an idea came to her and she looked at her surroundings. She was in a shopping area and a number of stores were still open despite the late hour. She walked along the street until she came to the kind of store she wanted, an electrical retailer. She knew exactly what she wanted so she was only in there for two minutes, and after that she found a public phone box, picked up the receiver and dialled a number.

'Hello, operator?' she said.

117

Chapter 11

Sam answered her cellphone. 'Special Agent Morrell.'

'This is Washington HQ, Special Agent Morrell, I'm just connecting you.' Then it went silent.

When Sam heard a click she repeated herself.

'I missed her by about five minutes.' The voice was female and sounded rather young, and rather peeved.

'Who is this?' asked Sam.

'Rachael Lamont,' replied the caller.

'Rachael! Go home right now, you don't . . .' Then what Rachael had said registered. 'You've seen Chloe?'

'No,' replied Rachael. 'But a guy who saw her saw me five minutes later and it confused him a bit. I've spent the last twenty minutes runnin' around the neighbourhood but I couldn't track her down.'

'Where are you?' Morrell asked.

'Wichita,' replied Rachael.

'What are you doing all the way up there?' asked Sam.

'Lookin' for my sister,' replied Rachael in a tone that conveyed perfectly what she thought about Sam's rather obvious question. 'And I missed her by five minutes, jeez am I pissed about that!'

'Listen to me, Rachael,' said Sam, her voice deadly serious. 'Go home, go home now. Your sister has fallen in with some very dangerous company and if you get near them then they'll kill you. Leave it to me to deal with this situation.'

118

'You don't understand,' said Rachael.

'No Rachael, *you* don't understand,' Sam shot back sternly. 'You don't know all the facts. This group abducted Chloe for a reason and she isn't in any danger from them but you will be if you go near them.'

'But . . .'

'No buts Rachael; go home right now!'

'But . . .'

'Didn't you hear me? Go home!' Sam barked.

'Agent Morrell,' Rachael grated the words down the phone, 'I shared a womb with Chloe for nine months. Do you have any idea what that means?'

That brought Sam up short as she was an only child. 'No, I don't,' she answered honestly.

'It means absolutely everythin',' said Rachael in a choked voice. 'Without Chloe I feel nothin', I am nothin'. I'd rather be dead than be without her. I'm gonna get her back.' And then the line went dead.

'Shit!' exclaimed Morrell, partly in frustration and partly in excitement.

'What's up?' Brody had heard only snatches of Sam's conversation as she was on the other side of the room getting them both a coffee.

'Rachael Lamont just called me from Wichita. Apparently someone saw Chloe and then saw Rachael five minutes later.'

'Can we trust this?' asked Brody.

'I don't know,' replied Sam. 'But I'm sure as hell gonna act on it!' And with that she got on the phone.

After phoning Agent Morrell, Rachael immediately got back in the car and took out her recent purchase, a radio tuner. Her mother's car already had a radio but what she had just bought was a little different and it was that difference that

119

had caused law enforcement agencies to be up in arms. This radio could tune into police-radio traffic information and the authorities had been trying for some time to get the device banned, restricted at the very least. Rachael put in the radio's earpiece and tuned in to the local police's frequency. The whole purpose of her phone call to Morrell was to find out more, as Rachael knew that the agent was holding a lot back with regard to Chloe's abduction. It seemed that Morrell was as certain as she was that Chloe was alive and unharmed, so that begged the question why was Chloe snatched? It seemed to Rachael that Morrell had been pursuing this group for some time, so Rachael was curious as to who these people were. Also there was Morrell's excitement that first morning when Rachael had told the Fed that the Winnebago's windshield was covered in tinfoil. Where did that fit in?

Rachael didn't have to wait too long before the police-radio operator started saying things that were of interest to her.

'Attention all units. We've just had a call from the FBI. Apparently a group that the Bureau is pursuing could possibly be in the Wichita area and the Bureau has asked us to keep a look out for them. They are probably driving a brand-new Roadtrek Versatile that could have licence plates from Texas, Oklahoma, New Mexico or Kansas. One of the vehicle's occupants is seventeen-year-old Chloe Lamont, who was abducted from New Mexico three days ago. She is described as five foot, four inches tall, one hundred and twenty pounds, blonde haired, pretty and wearing a dark brown leather jacket, dark blue denim jeans and white sneakers. If anyone should see either the vehicle or Chloe Lamont the FBI has ordered that local forces should only instigate surveillance from a safe distance and keep a track of their movements. The occupants of the vehicle are described as extremely dangerous and should not be

120

approached under any circumstances. Any sightings should be reported to police headquarters immediately, where the information will be passed onto the FBI. We are currently printing off photos and artist's impressions of the vehicle's occupants and will be circulating them straight away. Be advised that *all* law-enforcement agencies throughout the state have been put on full alert with regard to this matter. I repeat . . .'

That was interesting! thought Rachael. The FBI had alerted all the local police departments and yet had ordered them to keep their distance should the group be seen. Why? The group had been described as extremely dangerous but the police and the FBI had enough firearms to bring most people either to heel or take them down. Did the FBI want these people alive? If so, why?

It was somewhat frustrating for Rachael, for the information she had gleaned had only led to even more questions. All of Kansas had been alerted and Rachael suspected that the FBI had alerted neighbouring states as well. Who was this group that had taken Chloe? Rachael decided she needed more information; she had heard that photos and artist's impressions were being circulated among the Wichita police and she wanted to see them. However, she couldn't just ask the police for a copy so she was going to have to steal one. She pulled the car into the flow of traffic and went in search of a police patrol, earpiece still in place just in case any more information came over the airwaves.

Morrell and Brody were back in the car and heading north again. Their destination was now Kansas City, nearly two hundred miles away. Morrell had instantly discarded the idea of going to Wichita as by the time they had arrived there the quartet would be long gone. But she also knew that by the time she got to Kansas City the group would probably be further north; she was just trying to stay in touch with them at the moment.

An idea had occurred to her earlier, before leaving Oklahoma City; she had contacted Jim Wagner in New Mexico and asked for details about the car Rachael Lamont was driving. A cream-and-brown station wagon. Once she had taken down all the details she had alerted the states to the north to be on the lookout and to report Rachael's whereabouts to her should the girl be seen, but not to apprehend her.

'Are you gonna use Rachael to get to them?' Brody had asked.

'Not really,' replied Sam. 'But I do want to know where she is just in case. Remember, she claimed to have gotten within five minutes of Chloe in Wichita. Now, that could easily be a case of mistaken identity but we were convinced that Rachael would flounder around New Mexico and Texas and hey! She's even further north and possibly closer to Chloe than we are.' She took a sip of coffee before adding, 'As I said earlier, I'll take my leads any way they come. If Rachael does have some way of homing in on her sister then I'm going to use it to my advantage.'

'It can't hurt,' agreed Brody. 'We've got local law agencies on the lookout and if Rachael can get close then it'll make our job of pinpointing where they are a little easier.'

'Exactly my thinking,' nodded Morrell.

'When are you going to call more agents in on this?' asked Brody.

'When we get a positive sighting of them from the police,' replied Morrell. 'If I call in agents before that then we could easily get hindered in our pursuit. I'm an object of ridicule within the Bureau, remember?'

Brody shook her head sadly.

Now they were on the interstate, heading north at a steady eighty. Louise didn't worry about being pulled over

122

by any traffic cops as Sam had already alerted them that they were coming, giving them the make, model and licence plate of their car. Being able to speed was one of the perks of the job.

Brody couldn't really believe that this case had gone on for so long, that other members of the Bureau could be so blind. True, vampires were supposed to be just elements from old folklore, old European folklore, but the evidence was there. Okay, it wasn't concrete and compelling, but two and a half thousand rounds of ammunition doing nothing to these women? That surely should have created a large investigation that had a significant amount of Bureau resources poured into answering one important question.

How was that possible?

But it hadn't done; the Tacoma incident had been conveniently forgotten about, the agent leading the investigation had been ostracised by her colleagues and these women had been allowed to carry on killing with impunity.

Was it because people didn't *want* any of the old myths to be proved true?

Brody thought that there might be some truth in that. If vampires actually existed then what other bogeymen were also real?

She looked across at her partner, who was napping in the passenger seat. Sam was attractive; Louise was prepared to admit that Sam Morrell was 'hot' and she hoped that she would look as good when she reached that age. Early forties, good bone structure and long, blonde hair combined with inner strength. Women like Sam usually found good men to marry and raise a family with, but Sam hadn't done that. She probably would have left the Bureau some years ago in order to have those things in her life but she had sacrificed them because of this case. Louise was pretty sure of that, but what had been Sam's reward for that dedication?

Ridicule.

She had heard a lot of the stories when she was at Quantico and it saddened her that other members of the Bureau would regard Sam that way, especially as she was still an active agent. But things were a bit different for her now—she had a partner who not only knew what she knew but also believed it like she did. And she was getting more leads now than she'd ever had before. Brody was convinced that it would only be a matter of time before they caught up with the gang and dealt with them permanently. She did have a small itch at the back of her mind though, a feeling that catching up with them was going to be the easier half of the job.

Rachael was on the road again but she had only travelled as far as Junction City, some one hundred miles north of Wichita, before finding a motel for the night. Although she had woken up at seven that evening, because she hadn't slept properly the last two nights she found herself nodding off at the wheel. So she had found herself a motel and as she lay in bed she perused the printed sheets she had 'liberated' from a patrol car in Wichita earlier that evening. She had been fretting about how to go about getting the printouts until she had passed a Dunkin' Donuts. Just pulling into the parking lot was a patrol car with a single officer in it.

What was it with cops and donuts?

The policeman had walked into the store and had foolishly left his car unlocked. Rachael had been quick as lightning in pulling over and dashing over to his car. A quick look into it had shown her a few printed sheets on the passenger seat and she had recognised the photo of Chloe, the one she had given Agent Morrell, immediately. But then Rachael would have recognised Chloe from a hundred yards away on a moonless, pitch-black night. She had taken all the printouts, dashed back to her car and then casually pulled away into the flow of traffic; it had taken her less than two minutes. She had been sensing for some time that Chloe was getting further away and was anxious to follow her, so hadn't bothered looking at the sheets until she had arrived at the motel.

The first two sheets of paper contained photos and one of them was of Chloe. The other photo was of a dark-haired woman who looked to be in her early thirties and attractive. But there was something strange about the photo and it took Rachael a few moments to realise that it had been created on a computer. The only other thing on the page was a name, Margaret O'Hearn. Nothing else, no date of birth or place of origin, and that struck Rachael as odd. The next two pages were drawings, artist's impressions of women who looked to be about the same age as Margaret but there was only a description of hair colour and nothing else, no names, nothing. Rachael looked at these pictures and wondered why these three women had kidnapped her sister, and why exactly they were wanted by the FBI.

The second question was answered on the remaining sheet of paper. The women were wanted in connection with a string of killings dating back some years.

Not murders, killings. Rachael was unsure why *that* struck her.

Also there were the following strict instructions to any officer who may detect these women:

1. Do **not** under any circumstances approach at night.
2. Should the group be detected at night then discreet surveillance should be employed and movements tracked and reported to FBI Special Agent Samantha Morrell (cellphone number was given), who would assume control once she was present in the group's vicinity.

3. Should the group's whereabouts be discovered during daylight then the discovering officer was to contact FBI Special Agent Samantha Morrell (cellphone number was given), who would assume control once she was present in the group's vicinity.
4. The group used stolen vehicles to travel in. Vehicles could possibly be detected by <u>all</u> windows being blocked out using various items such as tinfoil, plastic bags, cardboard, etc. although that wasn't necessarily the case at night.
5. Do **<u>not</u>** under any circumstances approach at night.

Why shouldn't they be approached at night? And why was that iterated twice, with the 'not' emboldened and underlined? How dangerous were these women? Why did they block the windows? Why did they snatch Chloe?

More frustrating questions for Rachael. She could understand why Agent Morrell was keen to get her hands on them if they had been killing for years.

Killing, not murdering.

Rachael studied the photo of Margaret O'Hearn and the pictures of the other two women to commit them to memory, but who were they? The pictures could only tell her what these women looked like and nothing else. Her head nodded forward—time to sleep. She then switched off the light and buried her face in the pillow.

'Hang on Chloe, I'm comin'.' She was asleep within a minute.

The journey to Omaha passed without any worries for the group. Chloe was struck by a real lightness of mood in the van as she sat there listening to Maggie, Jen and Isa laughing and joking. Every now and then Jen would look at her and smile and every time Chloe would get a thrill of pleasure. She was one of them now, she had been ever since the morning they had snatched her out of the sunlight but it was only now that she truly realised, truly felt it.

'Oh yeah!' Isa suddenly said. 'Shouldn't our new sister here be equipped the same as us?'

'Yeah!' agreed Maggie, and Jen then dug into her holdall and pulled out a Beretta 9mm pistol and a couple of spare ammo clips; she passed the gun to Maggie.

Chloe's eyes widened in amazement as Maggie handed the gun to her with a small flourish. Chloe had never handled a firearm before, much less been given one.

'It doesn't hurt to have one,' said Jen. 'They sure were handy to have at Tacoma.'

Isa and Maggie murmured their agreement.

'Thanks!' Chloe managed to splutter. 'I've never fired a gun before though.'

'Not a problem,' said Maggie, smiling broadly. 'Once we get into the north fully I'll take you out where you can practise.'

'One thing I'm sure you're not aware of,' began Jen, 'is that guns can't hurt us.'

'What?' exclaimed Chloe, not quite believing she'd heard Jen correctly.

'We're bullet-proof!' Jen said, flashing a big grin.

'You gotta be shittin' me!' said Chloe.

Jen continued smiling as she pulled a gun out of her coat and shot Maggie in the chest at point-blank range. The gunshot was deafening and Maggie was propelled backwards by the bullet's impact. She hit the floor of the van hard and lay there; Chloe just sat there in total, wide-eyed shock.

'Fucking hell, Grandma!' Maggie yelled as she propped

herself up on her elbows. 'Give me some warning next time!' She was smiling as she said this, though.

'Has more impact if I don't,' replied Jen, inclining her head in Chloe's direction.

Chloe was just sitting there, staring in horrified fascination at the red stain on Maggie's tee shirt. 'Doesn't that hurt?' she asked in an awed whisper.

'Not really,' Maggie replied conversationally. 'But you do feel it hit you and you can feel the bullet in you as well. But that's easy to deal with, you just tense up.' Her face became a mask of concentrated effort and Chloe gasped as she saw the slug slowly emerge from Maggie's chest.

'Can anything hurt us?' Chloe asked Jen.

'Daylight hurts, direct sunlight kills,' replied Jen.

'Blood is our life, the night is our time and the sun is ever our bane,' Isa said quietly.

'Exactly,' said Jen with a serious expression. Then her face broke out into a broad smile and she handed Chloe the spare ammo clips. Maggie showed Chloe how to cock the gun and operate the safety catch. Chloe then tucked the gun into the inside pocket of her jacket and the clips went into another pocket.

The rest of the journey was spent with Maggie, Jen and Isa sharing reminiscences from the past, exploits and escapades that they, together with Caitlin, had got into. It made Chloe smile; she hadn't seen them this relaxed and it pleased her to think that she was partly responsible for the jocular mood they were in.

'Remember London?' Isa suddenly asked with a smile.

'How can I forget?' responded Jen with wide eyes and an even wider smile.

'What happened in London?' asked Chloe, casting puzzled eyes at Maggie, who was stifling her laughter and saying, 'Oh man, this one!'

'Well,' began Jen, glancing at Isa who was trying to stifle

128

her laughter. 'This was before Maggie joined us. Isa wanted to see London, I was curious too, and when we arrived there we were expecting this bustling city that we had heard so much about. Instead we find this cramped, filthy, miserable place and we couldn't understand it; we'd heard so much about England's capital. It wasn't until a few days later that we found out that the city had recently been ravaged by bubonic plague. That was why everyone was miserable.'

'But it was still a cramped and dirty place,' put in Isa.

'Tell me about it!' Jen rolled her eyes. 'Well, after a few boring days we decided to try and lighten the mood there a little.'

Isa was snorting now and her shoulders were jerking up and down; Maggie was the same and Jen was only just stifling her mirth.

'We had just fed,' Jen continued, 'and were feeling in good spirits and just for the hell of it we decided to set fire to a baker's shop.' Isa and Maggie were hardly able to contain themselves by this point. 'All we wanted to do was create a little bit of excitement in that area,' Jen carried on. 'However, no one responded to the fire and it began to spread.' She shook her head and looked out of the window. 'That little fire we started ended up burning a third of the city down.'

All three of them burst into gales of laughter at this and Chloe was smiling too. However, a suspicion had grown in her on hearing the story and so she asked, 'When exactly was this?'

'Oh, sixteen sixty-six,' replied Jen, wiping her eyes.

'You started the Great Fire of London?' Chloe's voice had gone up an octave.

'We didn't mean to!' protested Jen. 'We just wanted to create a little excitement to liven the place up!'

'And created a major moment in England's history!' Maggie laughed.

'It did the city a huge favour though!' Isa defended. 'Before the fire all the buildings were built right on top of one another. Raw sewage ran down the gutters and the place was just absolutely filthy. When they rebuilt after the fire they spaced everything out, made the whole place a lot cleaner and a hell of a lot better.'

'Yeah! We ended up staying in England for ten years after that,' said Jen.

Chloe just shook her head; Maggie, Jen and Isa appeared to be three ordinary women but a story like that hit home that these women had been around for quite some time.

Sixteen sixty-six? *Sheesh!* Then another thought occurred to Chloe.

'Uh, you guys weren't in Chicago in, say, eighteen seventy-one?' she asked.

'No, no, no!' laughed Isa. 'That wasn't us, we were in Maryland at the time. Or was it Virginia? Anyway, someone else started that fire!' Which set them all off laughing again.

Isa hadn't rushed and so the sky was lightening as they approached Omaha. Chloe was a little alarmed to see how close it was to sunup but the other three seemed unconcerned. Isa just looked at Jen and said, 'I think we should gear up and darken the van.'

Jen had nodded agreement and the girls went into action. Out of the holdall came towels, which they wrapped about their heads, then they put on tinted pilot's goggles and leather gloves. There was even stuff for Chloe to wear and she realised that this had once been Caitlin's. Once they had sorted themselves out they saw to the vehicle. As Isa was driving she only had one hand free and so it took longer to complete the job. Sixty-five seconds. Chloe found that her disquiet about the approaching dawn had been lessened some by covering her bare skin. That disquiet was further reduced by darkening the van.

They found a good spot in the industrial part of town, a

large wooden shed that was big enough to house four trailers side by side. Isa drove into it and saw that this place was hardly ever used and so parked their minibus in a far corner. By this time the sun had cleared the horizon and Chloe was surprised that she hadn't fallen asleep.

When she mentioned it to Maggie the other woman replied, 'You only fall asleep at sunup if you're ready to.'

'So we can move around during the daytime?' Chloe was stunned to learn this.

'Yes and no,' replied Maggie. 'We can move around after sunrise in order to find a place to bed down but the closer it gets to midday the more sluggish and lethargic we become; we are night creatures after all.'

'But we can get up in the middle of the day if there's the need,' added Jen quietly.

When Chloe saw the look the other three shared she knew they were referring to what had happened to Caitlin.

With the van parked and all the doors securely locked they bedded down for the day. Chloe gave Maggie a kiss before laying her head on the older woman's chest. The look of delight on Maggie's face when she did that sent her heart fluttering. She lay there listening to the *thump-thump* of Maggie's heartbeat and was asleep within thirty seconds. The other three were quick in following her.

Chapter 12

The sun had set again and as always Jen's eyes flew open. Normally she would rise up straight away but that dusk she felt lighter of mood than she had for many months. She lay there, head on Isa's chest, drawing light, lazy circles on her partner's stomach.

'Hmm, that feels real nice,' Isa purred. 'You haven't been in this good a mood for a long while. Am I gonna get lucky tonight?'

'Maybe,' Jen replied non-committally.

'Teaser,' Isa muttered sourly.

'Can you two keep your dirty talk for when you're alone?' said Maggie from across the van. 'We've got young ears present, you know.'

'Aw Mags!' Chloe complained. 'I was enjoying listening to that!'

All four of them laughed and Jen raised herself into a sitting position. When she looked across the van she found herself looking into Chloe's eyes, that were full of curiosity.

'Who are you, Jen?' the girl asked.

'Who am I?' asked Jen. It was a good question. 'I guess I'm some old broad who's well past her sell-by date.'

Both Maggie and Isa laughed at this.

'Sixteen sixty-six?' the girl pondered. 'How old are you?'

'How old is dirt?' asked Jen with a laugh. She then answered Chloe's question. 'I was born in fourteen fifteen.'

Chloe did some mental arithmetic and her eyes widened. 'You're nearly six hundred years old?' Her tone was one of awe.

'Thanks for reminding me!' said Jen sarcastically.

Chloe smiled as her eyes roamed up and down Jen's lithe body. Nearly six hundred years old and yet she only looked thirty-five, an incredibly alluring thirty-five too! Being a creature of the night certainly had its benefits.

'You were born in France?' Chloe asked and Jen nodded. 'How'd you get here then?'

'That's a long, long story,' Jen said.

'I'd like to hear it though,' said Chloe.

'It'd take all night.' Jen shook her head with a smile.

'A brief summary then!' Chloe laughed.

Jen looked thoughtful and Isa sat up and snuggled against Jen.

'Go on,' said Isa. 'Tell her.'

Jen gave Isa a smile and then said to Chloe, 'I was born in the small town of Labrède. It lies about fifteen miles south of Bordeaux, southwest France. As I think Isa has already mentioned, my family was a minor part of the nobility. It was when I was about seventeen that my mother and father decided that I was ready to marry and so paraded me, one evening, in front of a whole host of potential suitors.' Jen's eyes had that faraway look to them as she remembered things from over five centuries past, things from when she was human. 'There was, however, one uninvited guest there that night,' continued Jen. 'He was called Klaus Werlund, a Bavarian and a . . . creature, not a man. He was very taken with me, so taken with me that later that night he broke into my bed chamber, bit me and carried me off with him.' Jen stared at the floor; her face was pained as she remembered that. 'I was with him for six awful years. There I was, this innocent seventeen-year-old girl, privileged and looking forward to a life full of more privilege. Then suddenly I find myself living only at night with a thirst for human blood.' Jen stared at the ceiling then, lost in the past. She remained silent for a few moments before continuing.

'Klaus was a brute, there's no other word for what he was. He raped me whenever the feeling took him, which was most nights. He was an absolute monster who delighted in slaughtering his victims and it was because of that that I took so long in making my first kill. I did *not* want to be like him.' She looked directly at Chloe then and said, 'It took me fourteen months to make my first kill. I was on his wrist for over a year, feeding off him every night and after every feed he would slap me about and tell me that I should be so grateful to him for carrying me.' Her face turned bitter then and she added, 'If he hadn't turned me he wouldn't have had to carry me.'

'You were with him for six years?' asked Maggie, and Jen nodded. 'How did you get away from him? I never found that part out.'

Jen gave a vicious smile. 'Although he was a brute he did have some culture and as a result we frequently visited Paris.'

'Paris?' said Chloe, her eyes lighting up.

'Yes, although Paris in the fourteen hundreds wasn't the same as the more famous Paris of later centuries. It was smaller and had less in it but it was still a great place to visit at that time. Anyway, we had spent the last six years roaming all over France, with frequent visits to the capital. During that time I had finally learned to kill for myself although I didn't butcher my victims like he did. I also discovered that if I drank deeply one night I could skip a night before feeding again. Even after I got off his wrist Klaus still killed every night whether he needed to feed or not, he just liked killing. Anyway, after six years we were in Paris again and sleeping the day in the cellar of a tavern near the city's outskirts, secure behind these huge oak casks. That day I finally succeeded in doing something I had been trying to do for months: wake up and get up in the middle of the day.'

Chloe regarded Jen with wide-eyed amazement. When she slept in the day she slept like the dead.

'It was tough but I finally managed it. I dragged his sleeping body out into the cellar, carried him over to the stairs that went up to the large double doors that led onto the street. Then I heaved him up through the doors and out into the daylight.'

'Shit,' murmured Maggie. 'Next time I piss you off, Jen, could you tell me so that I can apologise?'

Jen gave a small smile and said, 'I hated him, absolutely *loathed* him. After throwing him out I ran up the stairs to close the doors, and felt my first touch of sunlight in six years. My skin started to blacken and smoke immediately and the pain was immense. But as I was closing the cellar doors I was treated to a wonderful sight: Parisians running around and shouting in consternation, because Klaus was lying in the middle of the street, thrashing and screaming and totally ablaze.' Jen's eyes were alight with the fire of triumph and Chloe could see just how much she hated the one who had turned her.

'When I got the doors closed I heard an explosion outside and I knew that I was finally free of him. Free of him but still a prisoner of the night.' She paused then, collecting her thoughts.

'I spent the next eighty or so years roaming around northern Europe, feeding every other night and sometimes stealing my victims' clothes when I wanted a change of garments. During that time I became incredibly miserable and wretched—the loneliness was unbearable. I was the only one of my kind that I knew of so in desperation I began to frequent taverns, not to find a victim but just to talk with someone. It helped a little but I still felt very lonely although I did discover another thing I could do. Gorging on a victim not only meant that I could skip feeding the next night but also that I could consume a little food and drink. This helped when I was in taverns, helped me blend in a little more, seem more . . . human. Then in . . .' She turned to Isa.

'Fifteen thirty,' Isa said.

'Fifteen thirty I found myself in the Tuscany region of Italy. I had been in the country since about the start of the century and I really liked it there; there was a friendliness to the Italians that I hadn't found in other Europeans. Anyway, by fifteen thirty I was in the Tuscan town of Grosetto and that was where I first laid eyes on this ugly moose here.' She indicated Isa, who just laughed and put her arm around Jen. 'The moment I laid eyes on her I fell for her, she was only about sixteen at the time but I had never seen anyone quite so beautiful. So I started talking to her and over the next few days, nights I mean, we really got chatty with one another.'

Isa interrupted then and said, 'What you have to understand is that on the night we first met I was being paraded in front of a lot of men I didn't like. My parents were looking to marry me off so I wasn't very happy and then in walks this stranger. She was dressed in an assortment of men's clothes and looked utterly strange and wonderfully different. I was intrigued and so wanted to talk to her.'

'And we talked,' continued Jen. 'During that time I was completely under her spell and that made me so miserable because I knew we couldn't really be friends. She was a lovely young girl and I was a hundred-year-old bloodsucker by that point. The problem I had was that when I was in Isa's company the loneliness I had felt vanished and I was actually happy for the first time since I was seventeen. As a result of this I remained in Grosetto for over three weeks,

136

the longest I had stayed anywhere since I had been turned. After three weeks the townsfolk realised that a fair number of people had been killed and that led to an air of fear and suspicion. I realised then that I would have to leave and leave very soon.' She paused then, her expression conveying some of what she felt all those years ago. 'That broke my heart, leaving Isa, but I had to leave else I'd eventually be discovered. I went to Isa one night to say goodbye and found that I couldn't talk; I was just too upset. Finally she asked me what's wrong and I said, "I'll show you".'

Isa took up the story then. 'I was very taken with Jen, she was unique, as in those days women were pretty much the property of men. Jen was independent though, and *strange*—she fascinated me; she was eloquent and intelligent but also deeply sad. I knew she was carrying some secret, some burden with her and I really wanted to help her. That night she came to say goodbye, she took me out into the town and we went to the poorer, less savoury part and it was there that she killed a man and fed from him in front of me. After that she broke down and wept, completely broken.'

'I was expecting her to run off into the night screaming,' continued Jen. 'Instead she wrapped me in her arms and comforted me. I clearly remember her saying over and over "you poor thing, you poor, poor thing". That made me cry even harder. She led me away from where I had killed and we found a quiet spot on the edge of town. There I told her practically everything: who I had been, what had happened to me, all the years I had wandered alone.' Jen then looked at Chloe and asked, 'Do you know what she did then?'

Chloe shook her head.

'She pulled the scarf away from her neck and tilted her head back. She asked me to make her like I was and when I asked why, she answered, "so that I can be with you for the rest of my life".'

Isa said the words in concert with her partner and Jen turned to Isa. Jen tried to say something but the words wouldn't come. Isa just kissed Jen's cheek and then said to Chloe, 'Jen had fallen in love with me when she first saw me and if I was perfectly honest with myself I fell in love with her straight away too. When she showed me what she was I wasn't disgusted or scared, I just felt incredibly sorry for her. I knew then that she was the reason for the large number of deaths in the town. I also realised that she was going to leave and I couldn't bear the thought of losing her. So I reasoned that if I were like her then we could stay together. Forever, it turns out.'

'I turned her then and there and we left Grosetto that night,' said Jen. 'Because Isa had willingly come over to be with me, had asked for it, I was never able to deny her a single thing. I carried her on my wrist for eight months but I didn't mind, she was everything to me and nothing was too much. Isa wanted to see lots of different places and I just agreed, so over the next two and a half centuries we travelled as far north as Stockholm, as far south as Constantinople and as far east as Moscow.' She turned to Isa and said, 'We saw a lot in that time didn't we?'

'Yes, we did!' agreed Isa. 'I wanted to see everything, which isn't possible really, but I gave it a damn good go!'

Jen laughed and carried on. 'Towards the end of the seventeen hundreds Isa said she wanted to visit the New World, as it was called then, and I just agreed although I had *huge* misgivings about that!'

Isa smiled and rolled her eyes. 'If I had known beforehand what I was letting us in for I would have stayed in Europe!' And she and Jen both laughed.

'Travelling over here was a nightmare for us,' said Jen. 'At that time George Washington was leading the War for Independence against the British. As a result the French supplied a lot of soldiers to aid him so there was a fair

138

amount of shipping between France and here. We stowed away on a cargo vessel, found a secure spot in the hold where we couldn't be found and we just stayed there until extreme hunger drove us out to feed. Because we were on a ship and didn't want to arouse any suspicion Isa and I would latch onto the same victim and drain him completely. It wasn't really enough for the two of us but we couldn't risk taking too many. After feeding we would toss our victim overboard and scurry back to our hidey-hole. I forget just how long that voyage lasted but it seemed like forever. When we finally made landfall we were absolutely ravenous and went on something of a rampage for the first few nights.'

'Where did you make landfall?' asked Chloe.

Jen and Isa both looked at each other then shrugged their shoulders.

'We have no idea,' said Isa. 'When we landed we were just focussed on slaking our thirsts. It was a long journey and we had denied ourselves in order to stay undetected. Once we hit land we spent the first few nights just roaming around and hunting.'

'Once we got back into our feeding routine of every other night we began to take notice of our surroundings,' Jen continued. 'We actually played our own small part in America's fight for independence by only feeding on British redcoats. Eventually the war ended and we carried on living as we had been in Europe, just roaming the countryside and feeding, perfectly happy with one another's company. The seventeen hundreds became the eighteen hundreds and it was then that Isa expressed a desire for a "daughter".' And Jen pantomimed quotation marks. She then looked to Maggie and said, 'That's when you came into our lives.'

'Eighteen twenty-two,' said Maggie with a fond smile. 'I remember it well.'

'Eighteen twenty-two!' exclaimed Chloe. 'When were you born?'

'Eighteen-o-four,' replied Maggie. 'So I guess that makes me over two hundred years old now.' She looked a bit startled at that and murmured, 'Where does the time go?'

'One thing that has surprised us, Maggie,' began Jen, 'is that you have remained with us all this time. As the decades rolled by we were sure that one day you would leave us and strike out on your own. When you turned Caitlin we figured that you would go then, but you didn't, you stayed.'

'Why should I leave?' asked Maggie. 'I love you and you me. You loved Caitlin when I turned her; life with you's great, so why give that up? I certainly wouldn't have survived without you when Caitlin was killed last year.'

She turned to Chloe and said, 'When I lost Caitlin I lost the will to live, the desire to feed; I just wanted to die. Isa wouldn't allow me to die though; she comforted me, fed me and carried me like a true mother. It's because of her patience and love that I'm still here.' The look she gave Isa then would have melted the coldest ice. Isa held her free arm out and Maggie crossed the van to hug the other woman.

'So you really *are* a family then,' said Chloe.

'Yes, we are,' replied Jen. 'And you're a part of it now, a sister, a daughter, a friend.' She too held out her arm and Chloe joined the trio, her family.

'Thank you,' said Chloe, her eyes glowing brightly.

No one said anything for a few moments, they just hugged one another and Chloe realised that the depth of love and loyalty that these women shared went far beyond that experienced by ordinary humans. All that they had was each other and they would always stand by one another. As Jen had just said and Maggie had said to her that first night after she had been turned, they were sisters, kin, family.

And that didn't mean the world to them. It *was* the world.

'That's a very brief history of Jen and Isa with a little Maggie thrown in,' said Jen.

'You've lived for so long,' said Chloe. 'Don't you ever get tired?'

'No.' Jen shook her head. 'Once Isa came into my life I had everything I needed. The love of a true partner does that for you.' And she cast a meaningful glance in Maggie's direction.

Both Chloe and Maggie blushed furiously.

'Let's get moving,' said Isa with a fond, broad smile. 'Where do you want to go to, Jen?'

Jen looked at the map and asked, 'Do you think you can make it to around Minneapolis by daybreak?'

'Shouldn't be too difficult,' said Isa as she started the van up.

As they headed onto the highway northwards Jen felt herself truly relax. She was sure that once they were in Minnesota they would be well out of the search area for Chloe.

Chapter 13

As soon as she had arrived in the Kansas City offices of the FBI, Morrell had gone into action. She knew that the group was some way north of her and she needed those areas fully aware of what could be in their territory. She and Brody began calling every police department and their emphasis was on missing persons; if three or more people had gone missing in a night then Morrell wanted to know about it.

'We won't find the bodies for at least a day or two,' she had told Brody. 'And I need to be closer to them than that.'

Brody had nodded understanding; she too realised that time was running out. Once Chloe became a fully-fledged member of the group then they'd become that much harder to track. As Sam had described it, 'One batch of kills in San Diego, California and the next could be in Portland, Maine.'

The Wichita PD had called Sam while she was journeying to Kansas City to say that no trace of the group had been found so far. Sam had told them that that was not surprising, you only realised they had been there when the bodies turned up. Sam told the Wichita PD that there was every chance the group had moved on so they might do better to try and detect their kills, if any had taken place.

Sam had only been in the Kansas City office for about twenty minutes when her cellphone rang. It was the Wichita PD again.

'Special Agent Morrell, this is Lieutenant Walt Greenbar of the Wichita police department here.'

'Go ahead, Lieutenant, any news?' replied Sam.

'Well, we've turned up a few dead bodies so far and four of them could be by your perps,' Greenbar informed her.

'How so, Lieutenant?' asked Sam, all interest.

'Well, two of them were killed separately and found in different parts of the city. Both victims had their throats cut. The other two victims were found in dumpsters in a quiet service road; they had both been garrotted with barbed wire.'

Garrotted with barbed wire? That was a new one!

'You could very well be correct there, Lieutenant,' Sam told him. 'That sounds like the hallmarks of the group I am chasing.' She wasn't going to tell him what the throat wounds were really for.

'The pathologist is due in any time now and we'll try and determine the cause of death. We'll investigate these homicides straight away and hopefully we can determine if they were carried out by your perps or whether the killers are more home grown. Whatever we discover we'll let you know,' said Greenbar.

'I greatly appreciate that, Lieutenant,' said Sam. 'Thank you for reacting so promptly to my request.'

'Not a problem, it's a pity that we can only be reactive to this group rather than proactive.'

'I know how you feel,' Sam said with a sigh. 'I know *exactly* how you feel.'

'Anyway, as soon as the pathologist has finished I'll let you know the results.'

'Thank you very much for your assistance, Lieutenant Greenbar, I'll be waiting for your call—hopefully very soon,' said Sam.

'I'll speak to you later.' And with that he hung up.

Sam and Louise studied the map.

143

'If they left Wichita shortly after feeding, then the next time they kill will be either in the Dakotas, Minnesota or Wisconsin,' Sam said quietly.

'How can you be so sure?' asked Brody.

'They're getting as far north as possible to get away from New Mexico,' said Sam. 'At the moment they're moving to get away from the abduction site, but I'm sure they don't realise someone's after them.'

'But Wichita to the northern states is a hell of a drive,' said Brody.

'Yes,' agreed Morrell. 'But they've got two nights to make the journey. I'm pretty sure that these girls feed every other night.'

'But Chloe—' began Brody.

'Four bodies were found in Wichita,' Sam interrupted with a bleak look. 'Chloe's feeding herself now. There'll be greater distances between kills.'

'We'd better get the northern states on full alert and then head on up there ourselves,' said Brody.

'Yes, we'd better.'

Rachael left the motel in Junction City shortly after eight o'clock the next morning. Although her bond with Chloe told her that her sister was somewhere north of her it wasn't like iron filings to a magnet. She couldn't 'home in' on Chloe and as a result she veered more eastward. Eight hours later Rachael wound up in Des Moines, Iowa and instantly knew that she was moving away from Chloe, who was still sleeping in Omaha at the time. However, Rachael was beginning to feel that she really needed to *know* what was going on, and to do that she would need to see Morrell's case file.

A hard task but not impossible.

As soon as she had arrived in Des Moines she began

144

searching for an internet café and as she was in a city she found one rather quickly. She logged onto the FBI's official website and began trawling through the various high-profile cases. She saw a wide array of wanted criminals, from the very famous Osama Bin Laden to the completely unknown Harmon Proctor, who was wanted for a string of murders and armed robberies across the central states. But there was no sign of the three women who had been killing their way across America for a number of years.

That's odd, thought Rachael. *Surely this would be a high-profile case too?*

It took her nearly an hour and a half of searching the FBI's website before she finally found the case. It turned out to be a complete waste of time as the website provided no more information than what she already had. Rachael was normally a sweet-natured girl but the string of epithets she then muttered would have got sailors blanching. She finished her quiet tirade with, 'Where's a good hacker when you need one?'

'That all depends on what you need hacking.' A voice sounded quietly by her shoulder.

It took Rachael about thirty seconds to climb back into her skin, such was the start she had been given. She rounded on the speaker ready to tear him off a strip or two but stopped when she saw him. He looked to be about nineteen years old and was a typical geeky nerd: bad clothes, bad skin, bad hairstyle and thick-lensed, thick-framed glasses. A definite hacker.

'I need information,' Rachael said to him.

'From the FBI?' queried the young man. 'You're treading on pretty thin ice there.'

'I know,' replied Rachael. 'But my twin sister was abducted four days ago by these women.' She indicated the pictures on the screen. 'I've got some information about them but it only poses more questions. I know my sister is

145

alive and the FBI agent who's searching for them believes that too, but I want to know why Chloe was taken. I think that this Fed knows and I want to know.'

'So you just want the case file?' he asked.

'Yeah,' replied Rachael. 'I want to know what Agent Morrell knows.'

'Shouldn't be too difficult,' he mused. 'And I can get it for you no problem as the FBI's security isn't that tight.'

'You've hacked them before?' asked Rachael.

'A time or two,' he admitted. 'No specific reason, just curiosity.'

'When could you get me the file?' asked Rachael quietly.

'Today,' he replied. 'There's a great diner on the north side of town, it's called Dom's, just ask anyone and they'll direct you straight to it.'

Rachael regarded him with wide eyes.

'Meet me there at about eight o'clock tonight. I should have all what you want by then. Oh, I'm Steve Harnessy by the way.' And he stuck out his hand.

'Rachael Lamont.' She shook his hand.

'See you at Dom's at eight then.' And with that he left.

Rachael stared after him, not quite believing her luck and feeling ever so suspicious. Just then another voice sounded behind her.

'Steve's the best, he'll get you the information you need.'

Rachael climbed back into her skin again and grated. 'Don't do that! My nerves are pretty shot as they are.' She saw that this speaker was a boy who looked slightly younger than she did but was a carbon copy of Steve Harnessy.

'Sorry,' said the boy. 'But you can trust Steve, he never stiffs a client.' And with that, he too departed.

Realising that she would be here for the night, Rachael set about finding herself a motel.

*

146

North and South Dakota, Minnesota, Wisconsin and Illinois had all been alerted and now Morrell and Brody were back on the road again. Their destination was Minneapolis—'Home of Caitlin Baker,' Morrell had murmured. Brody had inwardly winced at the coming journey, some four hundred miles, but agreed that it was absolutely necessary. They had to be as close to the group as possible. Once they were sighted, Morrell could then bring in other agents from the Bureau and then they would enter the final stages of this case.

As they were heading out of Kansas City Morrell told Louise what she suspected about the girls' feeding habits.

'I'm pretty sure they feed every other night,' she began. 'The only evidence I have for this is there aren't more bodies.'

Brody did some quick mental arithmetic and said, 'That's still over one hundred and eighty kills each a year.'

'I know,' replied Morrell. 'Scary, isn't it?'

'Sure is!' agreed Brody.

'Louise,' began Morrell, 'the USA has over eleven thousand firearm homicides alone each year, then add to that all the other homicides that happen and suddenly one hundred and eighty killings doesn't show up at all. One hundred and eighty times four doesn't even register so it's small wonder that these women have been able to do this undetected for so long. That's what I find scary.'

'Shit,' murmured Brody. 'You look at it like that and it brings it home to you just how violent our country is.'

'Yes,' said Sam. 'America is the perfect place for these girls.'

'Do you hate them?' asked Brody. It seemed a silly question but Louise was interested to learn Sam's view of this group.

'No, I don't,' replied Morrell. 'In fact, I have some kind of sympathy for them.'

147

'Sympathy?' Brody was shocked.

'Yeah, they're creatures, Louise, creatures just following their nature. They roam around and feed. That's all they do really.'

'But they kill people!'

'So do people,' replied Sam. 'And these girls kill for a very good reason—to survive. As I've said before, they are killing but they're not murdering, they're feeding.'

'Doesn't justify the killing though,' Brody argued.

'Not to a human perspective it doesn't,' Morrell agreed. 'But then we humans are arrogant. When a lion kills a zebra on the African plain we say that's just nature. But if that lion was to kill a human then we would immediately kill the lion and we wouldn't even try and justify that.'

Brody was silent for a few moments; she found herself agreeing with Sam on that point. 'That's not going to stop you from killing these women though, is it?'

'No it isn't, Louise,' Sam replied with a sigh. 'After all, I'm just an arrogant human like everybody else. Plus it's my job to stop them.'

Brody looked across at her partner and saw that Sam still wore the mask of steely determination, but it couldn't hide the weariness. Ten years!

'One thing that puzzles me Sam, is their age,' said Brody.

'How so?' asked Sam.

'Well, you say that Maggie O'Hearn disappeared when she was eighteen and Caitlin Baker was twenty when she vanished and yet they both look about thirty-five now. I thought vampires didn't age at all.'

'According to fiction they don't,' replied Sam. 'However, what we're dealing with here is the reality and the rules are probably different. These girls do continue to age after being turned but only until they reach their thirties.'

'Why though?' asked Brody.

'Milf,' replied Sam.

148

'Milf?' Brody was confused.

'Yeah, M-I-L-F.' Sam spelled it out. 'It's an acronym.'

'What's it stand for?'

Sam gave Louise a look that could only be called rude. 'Mother I'd like to Fuck.'

'Sam!' Brody admonished 'There's no need for th. . .' and then the penny dropped.

'Oh, I get it, the older women thing.'

'That's what I think,' agreed Sam. 'When you're in your mid-thirties you still have your youthful good looks only they're now augmented by a bit of maturity. One thing all the witnesses I've spoken to who've seen these women say is how fantastic looking, how alluring they are. I suspect that they are like that on purpose in order to hunt us easier.'

'You call them creatures Sam. You're not saying that they're *natural* creatures are you?' Louise was a little horrified.

'You know, the longer I pursue these girls the more I come to believe that they're meant to exist, that there's a reason for them being here. And they are quite peaceable really. Apart from Tacoma, which was when I attacked them, you don't realise that they're even there.'

'But all their victims!' Brody protested.

'Hunger,' said Sam. 'Predator and prey. The law of the savannah. They only kill to feed. The rest of the time you don't hear from them.'

'But if they are natural creatures, what's their purpose in life?' asked Louise.

'I thought that was obvious,' replied Sam. 'To keep our numbers in check.'

'They're not doing a very good job if that's the case,' Louise countered.

'That's because there isn't enough of them. They are very powerful but they do have that one Achilles' heel, sunlight, which is why they're so secretive. Maybe it's made them too cautious and as a result of that their numbers aren't up to what they should be.'

Louise considered this and realised that Sam could very well be correct in her theory, which made her feel uncomfortable. She was about to continue the discussion but just then Sam's cellphone rang.

'Special Agent Morrell,' she answered.

'Hello Agent Morrell, it's Lieutenant Greenbar from Wichita here. The pathologist has just finished his autopsies on the four bodies we think were the work of your perps. Both the garrotting and the knife wounds turned out to be post-mortem and in all four cases the corpses were missing around eight pints of blood.'

That was all Sam needed to hear. 'Thank you for that, Lieutenant,' she said. 'You can chalk those four killings up to my girls.'

'You're sure?' asked Greenbar.

'Absolutely positive, Lieutenant,' replied Sam.

'It's the missing blood, isn't it?' guessed Greenbar. He was about to carry on but Sam interrupted him in a kind, gentle voice.

'Lieutenant, I can tell you if you *really* want to know.'

There was a few moments' silence on the other end before Greenbar replied, 'It's your case, Agent Morrell, and I shouldn't interfere.'

'Thank you for your prompt action, Lieutenant, you've aided me greatly,' said Sam.

'I hope you catch them, and soon, Agent Morrell. We may speak at a later date.' And with that he hung up.

Sam pressed 'end' on her phone and then turned to Brody.

'Positively confirmed,' said Morrell. 'They *were* in Wichita, so let's get to Minneapolis with all speed. I want to get in front of them now.'

Keeping the car at a steady eighty, Brody drove north towards the Minnesotan capital.

Rachael arrived at Dom's at about ten to eight that evening and the place surprised her. She was expecting a fast-food joint but Dom's was more on the way to being a proper restaurant. She found herself a table in the corner and sat down. Thirty seconds later a waitress came up and handed her a menu.

'Would you like anything to drink?' she asked Rachael.

'A coffee please,' replied Rachael.

'Regular or decaf?'

'Regular please,' Rachael answered.

'Columbian, Kenyan, Puerto Rican or Java?' asked the waitress.

Rachael burst out laughing; she wasn't expecting this much choice from a cup of coffee. She controlled her mirth and answered, 'Columbian will be fine.'

The waitress smiled at Rachael and then went to fetch the coffee. As she was sitting there sipping her drink she saw Steve Harnessy arrive; a quick check of her watch showed that it was eight o'clock exactly, very prompt. He stood at the entrance and scanned the seating area. Rachael raised her arm to attract his attention and he made his way over to her. She noticed he was carrying a large brown envelope and her heart started fluttering: did he have it?

'Hi there,' he said, sitting down.

'Hi,' replied Rachael. 'Any luck?'

'I downloaded and printed off everything there was,' he replied, handing over the envelope. 'Whether it's what you're after or not is a whole other ball game.'

'Thank you,' said Rachael, her voice conveying her gratitude.

'*De nada,*' said Steve, waving his hand dismissively.

The waitress approached their table again and she had another cup of coffee in her hand. 'There you go Steve, one cup of Java decaf.'

'Thanks Simone,' Steve said with a smile.

'You havin' your usual?' asked Simone.

'Sure,' replied Steve and the waitress turned to take Rachael's order.

Rachael had scanned the menu while she had been waiting and had seen that this place did the usual diner food you found everywhere and so opted for the steak.

'Would you like chips, rice or jacket potato with that?' asked Simone.

'Chips?' Rachael was incredulous.

Steve interrupted then and said, 'Dom, the chef, hails from England and over there they call fries "chips". They're a bit different but I think they're better than fries.'

'Oh,' said Rachael. 'In that case I'll have chips then.'

The waitress smiled, took the menu and went to give the chef the order.

'Strange hack that one,' Steve commented. 'Normally the FBI has a number of firewalls around the stuff they don't want you to see. The firewalls are pretty easy to get around but that one was even easier.' He took a sip of coffee and added, 'I've also burnt the info onto a CD-ROM for you as well as doing the printouts.'

'Thank you,' said Rachael. 'How much do I owe you for this?'

Steve just gestured to the table and said, 'You're buyin'.'

'Thank you!' Rachael was stunned; the food in this place was very reasonable.

'Normally I'd charge a lot more but as you're tryin' to find your sister I'm doin' my good deed for the day.'

During the meal they made small talk and Rachael told him about her hometown of Fulfilment. Steve seemed interested as he had been born and raised in Des Moines and had never ventured out from it. Towards the end of the meal Rachael noticed a young woman approach their table and the look she gave Rachael was venomous. Although Rachael wasn't very world-wise she nevertheless knew instinctively that this was Steve's girlfriend so she raised the envelope and said, 'Don't mind me, sister. This is strictly business and I'm from out of town.'

The girl's expression went from venom at Rachael to annoyance with Steve. 'Steve, you are gonna get into real trouble one of these days!'

'Hiya Shelly!' Steve greeted her with a big smile and moved to the next seat so that she could sit down. Once she was seated, he introduced her. 'Rachael, this is my good lady Michelle Ronson. Shelly, this is Rachael Lamont.'

'Hi!' said Michelle. Her expression was tight and her smile did not reach her eyes.

'Hello there,' Rachael replied, laying her New Mexico accent on thick to emphasise that she was not trying to move in on Steve.

'Rachael's twin sister was kidnapped four days ago and she's trying to find out why,' Steve explained. 'She suspects that the FBI knows so I went and got her the case file.'

'You hacked into the Bureau!' Michelle hissed. 'Are you nuts?'

'Ahh, take it easy,' said Steve. 'Sears and Roebuck have got better firewalls than the FBI. If the Feds don't want people snoopin' in then they should make their security tighter.'

Rachael got the feeling that this was a well-worn argument between the two of them but didn't want to hear it in any case. So she put four ten-dollar bills on the table to pay for the meal and said, 'Thank you for doing this Steve, I'm gonna head off now and do some reading.'

'Sure thing, Rachael,' replied Steve. 'I hope you find your sister.'

'So do I,' replied Rachael. 'So do I.'

'You got a place to stay tonight?' he asked.

Rachael saw Michelle's back stiffen and expression turn black as night. Rachael felt a bit sorry for her—being *that* possessive would get rather tiresome. 'Sure have,' she replied. 'I'm at the Motor Inn on the edge of the city.'

'I know it,' said Steve, nodding. 'Pretty reasonable place I've heard.'

'Yeah, it's within my meagre budget,' Rachael laughed. 'Thank you once again and all the best for the future.' And with that she left the restaurant and headed back to her motel.

As she walked along the streets she could feel that Chloe was on the move again, somewhere west of her and heading north. Rachael was of a mind to follow but she had spent most of the day driving and couldn't face more hours on the road without getting some sleep first.

Besides, there was Morrell's case file to read and Rachael was fervently praying that it would answer her questions and not just give her more.

Chapter 14

On the fifth morning since being snatched out of the sun, Chloe had bedded down with the others in a quiet district of Mankato in southern Minnesota. Rachael was a couple of hours from waking up in Des Moines and, unbeknownst to the girls, Morrell and Brody were arriving in Minneapolis.

'How do you feel, Louise?' Sam asked.

'Absolutely bushed,' replied Brody.

'Good, me too,' said Sam. 'Straight to bed for both of us and we can be awake and fresh before our girls get up. Remember, they'll kill tonight.'

'But where?' asked Brody.

'That's up to the locals to tell us,' replied Sam. 'Hopefully they won't be too far away and hopefully the locals'll latch onto their kills quickly.'

'Hopefully, hopefully, hopefully,' Louise laughed.

'Yeah, I know.' Sam laughed as well. 'But Christ! I need a good break on this.'

'Well,' said Louise with a big grin, '*hopefully* we'll get it.'

Sam laughed again and the two women checked into a motel.

There was a knock at the door; it was followed thirty seconds later by another knock. Rachael looked at the door but made no move to get up and see who it was—this morning she didn't want to do anything. There was a third knock followed by, 'Rachael?'

The voice sounded female but Rachael didn't care, she stayed where she was, sitting on the edge of the bed.

There was a fourth knock, loud and insistent, followed by 'Rachael, please answer the door.'

Rachael got to her feet and shuffled to the door; she opened it slightly and peered out into the morning light. It took Rachael a few moments to recognise the caller; it was Michelle Ronson, Steve Harnessy's girlfriend.

'I was calling to apologise about my snippy attitude last night,' she began apologetically. 'You see I . . .' Then Michelle saw the state of Rachael's face, eyes red-rimmed from crying, the expression one of utter dejection.

'Oh God Rachael! What's wrong?' Michelle had gone from sincere apology to sincere concern.

Rachael tried to answer, tried to tell Michelle that nothing was wrong, that everything was okay. Instead she burst into fresh tears.

Michelle took charge then. She gently but forcibly pushed the door open further and then entered the motel room, ushering Rachael ahead of her. She closed the door and then enfolded the other girl in a warm hug. Michelle didn't know what was wrong but she could clearly see that Rachael was distressed and so instinctively comforted her. She led Rachael to the bed where they sat down. Michelle held Rachael close and didn't ask anything until the tears were through. Finally Rachael was able to get herself back together and she gently moved out of Michelle's embrace, smiling her gratitude.

'What's up, Rachael?' Michelle asked.

'Chloe's not comin' back,' Rachael said simply and Michelle guessed that Chloe must be Rachael's twin sister. 'Also, the FBI agent that's after them is goin' to kill them all.'

'Why?' asked Michelle, shocked at this last statement. Rachael looked like she was about to burst into tears again but controlled herself and just gestured to the printouts that lay on the bed.

Michelle gathered the papers into a pile and then looked to Rachael, who just indicated with her head that Michelle should read. Michelle was about to when she heard a loud rumble emanate from Rachael's stomach. She made a decision then.

'I can read this later, first thing we have to do is get some food inside you.'

'I'm not hungry,' replied Rachael dully.

'I don't care,' replied Michelle. 'You're still going to eat something.' And with that she gently pulled Rachael to her feet and led her over to the motel's small diner.

They ate breakfast in silence, Rachael eating mechanically whilst Michelle skipped through the case file taking in all the pertinent points. It was all there, the two multiple killings in Ohio and Indiana that had started the investigation, the series of killings across the northern states, the cataclysmic gunfight in Tacoma. The discovery of the O'Hearn family portrait, the search through the missing-persons database to discover Caitlin Baker. The countless other killings that had taken place over ten years, the Brunswick pathologist's report, the death of Caitlin Baker.

And Samantha Morrell's personal point of view about these women.

Michelle read it aloud although quietly so no one sitting nearby could hear. ' "These women have lived for over one hundred years at least although they still look to be in their mid-thirties. Bullets do nothing to them, save piss them off and they are extremely adept at blending in unnoticed. As for the killings they carry out? They are not murdering, they are feeding." ' The last three words were spoken in an awed whisper.

'And Chloe's one of them now,' said Rachael in a small voice.

'Oh Rachael!' Michelle reached out and gently held Rachael's hand.

'It explains a lot of things,' said Rachael, mostly to herself as she stared out of the diner windows. 'Why law enforcement should *not* approach them at night, why the windshield was covered with tinfoil, why smoke was pourin' out of Chloe that first mornin'.'

She then looked directly at Michelle, tears glistening in her eyes.

'My sister's a vampire now and she's not comin' back.'

Michelle was shocked to silence. Vampires were supposed to be fictional creations and yet all the evidence she had read had convinced her that they were very real. Finally she asked, 'What are you going to do?'

'I should just head on back home,' replied Rachael. 'But what's Fulfilment without my sister? Just an empty backyard in the middle of nowhere.' Then her face screwed up as she fought back more tears. 'And how can I look Momma in the eye knowin' what I know now? It's written in the Bible "he who increases knowledge increases sorrow". I know exactly what they're on about now.'

Michelle gathered all the printouts together and pushed the pile towards Rachael. The CD-ROM was on top of the pile and Rachael picked it up and handed it to Michelle saying, 'What you do with this information is up to you but I'm gonna stay out here and try and find her before Morrell does.'

'Why?' asked Michelle.

'To say goodbye. To tell her I love her. Chloe's lost to me now but I would like to see her one more time.'

Michelle pocketed the CD, looked directly at Rachael and said, 'Be careful, Rachael.'

'I will.'

158

'And best of luck.'

Rachael smiled back and got up from her seat, picking up the pile of printouts. As she made to walk away she bent down and kissed Michelle's cheek.

'Keep Steve on a tight leash otherwise he's gonna land in serious trouble one day.'

'Tell me about it,' replied Michelle wryly. 'You keep safe, Rachael, and I hope you find Chloe.'

Rachael gave a sad smile and then left the diner. Chloe was somewhere north of her and that's where Rachael had to head.

Darkness had fallen and the quartet had risen lazily, no hurry in them. There wasn't any of the urgency to feed and move on as there had been the previous nights so Chloe took time to wander away a little and just feel the night. She opened herself up fully and let the sensations just wash right through her; she understood then what Maggie meant that first night they had met. If she had done this when she was still human then the darkness would have blinded her, the silence would have deafened her. For humans the night was dark and silent, for her kind it was bright and loud. She tuned in to the myriad of pulsing signals that filled the night, from the tiny, almost inaudible ticking of the small rodents that scurried about, through the louder bumping of raccoons and other larger creatures up to the drumbeat thump that signalled humans.

Prey.

Chloe shucked off her jacket and pulled her tee shirt over her head to stand there topless. As she felt the cool night air play over her skin she shuddered with pleasure and wondered what it would feel like to truly be one with the night, to completely give herself over to it. She kicked off her trainers and sent her jeans and panties down to the ground before stepping out of them, then she removed her socks. Standing there fully nude, with the gentle breeze washing over her and the sensations of the night coursing through her, it was all she could do not to cry out in pure elation.

'Quite something, isn't it?'

Chloe turned her head to find Isa standing nearby, nude also.

'Sure is,' she responded. 'I don't think I've ever felt this alive before in my whole life.'

'I'd be surprised if you had,' chuckled Isa. 'I don't think humans are capable of feeling what we feel. Not truly anyway.'

Chloe stared at the ground, her toes flexing in the dirt.

'What's that I can feel through my feet?' she asked Isa. 'It's like a heartbeat.'

'That,' replied Isa, her eyes lighting up, 'is the pulse of the very world itself. All natural creatures can sense it. All except humans of course, they've moved too far from their place in nature.'

'We're natural creatures?' Chloe was absolutely stunned by this revelation.

'Of course we are!' replied Isa. 'Man has taken himself out of the food chain for the most part. He considers himself safe from predators now but we were created to hunt humans, feed off them. And because of the way we live, quietly in the shadows, always on the move, never staying in any one place too long, we're able to successfully live according to our nature. Man has no knowledge of our existence—to him we're just a fiction.'

'How long have our kind been around?' asked Chloe.

'I have no idea,' replied Isa. 'But I suspect that we have been around as long as humans have. And our ancestors hunted theirs.'

'Cool,' said Chloe. Somehow that felt right to her.

'Anyway,' said Isa, 'the night is young and I don't know about you but I'd like to feed.'

'I'm right with you there, sister!' said Chloe with a big smile.

'We're right by a town,' continued Isa, 'so there's no shortage of prey, but choose your target carefully. As strong as we are, always remember that we hunt the most dangerous animal on the planet. Arouse their suspicion too much and they'll come hunting us, and they'll hunt during the hours of daylight when we're at our most vulnerable.' Isa looked squarely at Chloe and said, 'Focus on the night, focus on the humans. A small group, isolated from everyone else. Four or less, Chloe, four or less.'

Chloe closed her eyes and reached out into the night with her senses, the drumbeat thump of humans loud in her ears. She narrowed her focus down and skirted the edges of the town, looking to the surrounding countryside for small, isolated groups.

'There are several small groups of people out there,' Chloe reported.

'Four or less, Chloe.'

Chloe turned her head to the voice and saw Jen and Maggie walking to join them. They were also nude and their eyes were bright, lit by a fire stoked by the bloodlust that burned within them. Chloe regarded Maggie, Jen and Isa, her pack-mates, and realised she had never seen anything quite as beautiful as these creatures.

'Four or less, Chloe,' said Maggie, her sister, her life-mate to be.

'I need to get closer to find which group is really isolated,' she told them.

'Lead us out then, Chloe,' said Jen with a gentle, encouraging smile.

Chloe smiled in return and started walking into the darkness, but not like a human would. Instead her upper

161

body was bent forward slightly, her step was on her toes only and as she walked her upper body stayed still. She upped her pace into a gentle jog, the other three following behind. Anyone who saw them then would have instinctively recognised what was happening.

They were *hunting*.

Chloe still hadn't decided which target to go for but she upped her pace again into a gentle lope, long strides that ate up distance, and her three sisters matched her speed. Chloe wanted to close the distance a little more, check which targets were truly isolated before committing to one.

On the outskirts of Mankato, in the Minnesotan countryside, were a fair number of folk. Wilson Lockhart was loading the back of his pick-up truck with planks of wood for the workshop he was building in his back yard. Helping him were his two best buddies, Louis Johnson and Dale Stonebrook.

In another part, high-school pals Timothy Gadge and Troy Evers were out by Paulson Lake with their girlfriends. 'Lake' might be a bit too grand a word for the body of water, but 'large pond' wouldn't have done it justice either. They had travelled there in Tim's car and both boys were hoping that their girlfriends were in good moods as they were of a mind for some serious making out that night.

Julie Minors and Alannah Freesh were walking home along a wooded, unlit road. Although it was dark neither woman worried about their safety as they were both crack shots, had permits to carry concealed weapons and each woman had a .38 Smith and Wesson tucked in an armpit holster. Anyone tried it on with them and they'd regret it.

Lester Parks, Reece Argyle, Jack Paley and Harlan Bautz were going for a night out. They were all in good spirits as they had been paid that day and the evening of payday meant them going to their local bar, sinking a few beers and playing a few frames. They were responsible men and

162

always left their cars at home whenever they went out for a drink. Besides, the mile or so walk to and from the bar was good exercise.

None of these people had any idea that death stalked the countryside on swift feet that night.

Chloe had led them for a minute or two at an easy lope through the lightly wooded terrain, her senses probing forward. All the possible targets were viable but as she closed the distance one group was looking totally ideal. Chloe looked back over her shoulder and the other three saw certainty in their younger sister's eyes. Their eyes lit up even further and Chloe committed to the target; they would not stop until they had brought their prey down. The gentle, easy lope Chloe had been travelling at suddenly changed and they were flying, literally flying over the ground. Chloe had never felt anything like this before, the sheer *thrill* of it! She had locked onto the group and was now bearing down upon it at full speed; Maggie, Jen and Isa were right behind her, closing in for the kill.

'Hey Wilse! How much more to go?' Dale Stonebrook asked.

'Not much,' replied Wilson Lockhart. 'Just these planks and that bag of cement over there.'

'Great!' replied Louis Johnson. 'How about we play a few games of poker once we get this lot offloaded?'

'Sounds like a good idea to me,' said Wilson. 'I don't know what it is but I sure feel lucky tonight!'

'Hey Reece, you gonna let me seven-ball ya again tonight?' laughed Lester Parks.

163

Reece Argyle just gave him a hard look and said, 'Very funny, you just got lucky last week, that's all.'

'As I remember,' said Harlan Bautz, 'Lester spent all that night chatting that broad up and got absolutely nowhere with her. I'd say that he didn't get lucky!'

Reece, Harlan and Jack Paley all laughed and Lester shrugged his shoulders and muttered, 'Come on guys, you know what some women are like. They just can't see a good thing when it's right in front of them.'

'Hey Lester!' called Jack. 'Think you'll get lucky tonight?'

'Sure!' replied Parks. 'I always get lucky!'

'Okay Mister Gadge, I'm ready now,' said Lucinda Fremont in a *very* false voice.

'Ladies and Gentlemen!' yelled her boyfriend Tim in the style of voice used by a circus barker. 'The one, the only, Lucindaaa Freeemoooont!' And Lucy stepped into the headlight beams of Tim's car.

Troy Evers and Mary-Lou Hopkin clapped and cheered and for extra effect Tim turned the headlights onto full beam.

'Christ!' exclaimed Lucinda as she threw her arms up in front of her face to cut out the blinding glare.

Tim had parked his car near the lakeshore a short distance from a stand of trees and he had switched his headlights onto full just as the quartet of predators came bursting out into the open.

As soon as the headlights illuminated the four hunters a primitive memory surged forward in the minds of Tim, Troy and Mary-Lou. The moment they saw the four they *knew* they were in mortal peril, instinct kicked in and a mass of adrenaline was dumped into their systems. With terrified screams the three of them turned on their heels and *ran*.

Lucinda, on hearing the screams, turned around and

164

caught a brief glimpse of a naked girl as Chloe barrelled into her at full tilt. The force of the impact sent Lucy flying backwards, with Chloe firmly gripping her, over the hood of the car to smash head first through the windshield. Lucinda's screams were brief, gargled and accompanied by a horrid growling sound as Chloe tore at Lucy's neck with her teeth.

As Chloe crashed through the glass Maggie bore left and zeroed in on her target, Troy Evers. Jen bore right and went after Timothy. Isa carried straight on, running over the car with three strides, hood, roof, trunk. She hit the ground without breaking her stride and homed in on Mary-Lou who was wearing sneakers and was only a yard or two behind Timothy Gadge.

There was an agonised cry as Maggie brought down Troy and sank her teeth in. Isa pounced like a leopard when Mary-Lou stumbled and crashed to the ground. She screamed once, briefly.

Timothy Gadge was the quarterback for the high-school football team and was extremely proficient at running. Running for his life gave him more impetus than ever before but it did him no good. Despite the fact that he had a head start, Jen was almost on his heels after just fifteen yards, such was her speed. Tim could sense she was right behind him and so employed the moves he used so expertly on the football field, swerving left and then right. Jen matched him every time though and she anticipated his next dodge and pounced. As Tim swerved to his left he felt a heavy weight smash into his back and felt strong arms and legs wrap around him. He staggered on for a few more steps and then cried in agony as Jen's teeth sank into his neck. He crashed to the ground and rolled but Jen had fastened tight to her prey and was not letting go.

It took less than a minute from when Tim had switched his main beams on for all four teenagers to die.

165

Maggie lay there on the grass, the corpse of her victim lying close by. Nearby she could hear the occasional belch from one of the others; they had all gorged deeply this night and like all animals that do so they were lying quietly afterwards. Normally they would clear up after themselves straight away, but Maggie was tuned to the night and could sense that the nearest people were a good distance away, no chance of being discovered. Chloe had chosen her target well and this filled Maggie with pure pride—to do so when she was so young and so new to this was astounding. Maggie giggled to herself and then sighed with pure contentment. It was on nights like these that the real reward of being what she was was truly felt. She stretched languidly, delighting in the feel of her muscles straining. She lay there for several more minutes before slowly raising herself into a sitting position. She looked across the clearing; nearby, Isa was also sitting up and wiping her mouth and chin.

'Good hunt,' she said.

'Sure was,' replied Maggie. 'We should do this more often.'

'Yeah,' agreed Isa. 'But not doing it often makes it more special when we do.'

Maggie couldn't argue with the logic of that. She saw Jen slowly walking across the clearing, dragging her victim behind by one leg.

'Okay girls,' said Jen in a lethargic tone. 'Let's get this cleaned up.'

Isa stood up and grabbed her victim's ankle.

Maggie looked over to where Chloe was, lying on the hood of the car, and saw that the girl was slowly getting to her feet. Maggie sighed and got up herself. The four of them dragged their victims together.

'How shall we cover this one up?' asked Maggie.

'Most obvious solution,' said Isa, 'is to put the bodies in the car and then heave the car into the lake.'

166

'We'll do that then,' said Jen. 'Hopefully it'll be deep enough, it should take some time before they're discovered.'

With that, the four of them put the bodies into the back of the car, jamming them behind the front seats.

'Three, two, one, lift!' counted Jen. She and Isa were at the front of the car; Maggie and Chloe were at the rear. The car lifted off the ground with ease and the four of them walked with it to the water's edge.

'One,' said Jen and they began to swing the car back and forth, 'two, three!' And they heaved it outward.

The car hit the water some twenty feet out and the wash from the impact lapped onto the shore. There was the sound of bubbling as water displaced the air in the vehicle and the car sank beneath the surface in under a minute.

Maggie regarded the sinking vehicle and stretched luxuriously again. A quick glance to her right showed Chloe doing the same.

'See you back at the van,' said Jen over her shoulder to Maggie as Isa slowly but firmly led her partner off into the darkness.

'It's absolutely disgusting at your age,' Maggie called after them and she laughed as a dual 'fuck off' came back at her. She turned to Chloe, smiled and then pulled the girl into a fierce hug. 'Well done, Chloe, that was a brilliant hunt!'

'I'm glad you liked it, I certainly did!' replied Chloe, laughing. She had *never* felt this alive before.

'We haven't done that since . . .' And then Maggie went very silent but Chloe knew what she was going to say.

'Since before Caitlin died?' She said it with as much gentleness as she could muster.

'Yeah,' said Maggie in a quiet voice. 'Our last hunt with Caitlin was the night before she was killed in actual fact.'

Chloe gently cupped Maggie's cheek and tenderly kissed her, then she took Maggie's hand and led them slowly in

167

the direction of the van. They walked in silence for some minutes, each of them lost in their own little world; Chloe's was filled with images, sensations and the pure elation that she had truly *become*, Maggie's was one of sweet melancholy for the love she had lost.

Maggie was brought out of her reverie when Chloe suddenly lay down on a patch of grass and gently pulled Maggie with her. Maggie was completely taken by surprise at this; she was hoping that Chloe would look at her in that way but wasn't expecting it this soon.

'Chloe, I . . .' began Maggie.

'Sssh!' said Chloe, putting a finger to Maggie's lips. 'Do you know what to do?' Maggie nodded. 'Show me.'

Chloe had never had a sexual experience before. She had let one or two boys fondle her but nothing more than that and kissing. What Maggie introduced her to was something beyond her imagining. Maggie's soft lips caressed her skin in a way no hand could ever match and Chloe just lay back and let Maggie take her where she would. Maggie kissed and caressed her all over and when she finally laid face-to-face, Chloe cut into her wrist with a thumbnail, drawing just a little blood. She offered the cut to Maggie, who put it to her lips and at the same time opened a small wound in her neck for Chloe. The two of them completely shared themselves with the other, shared their bodies, shared their blood. When Chloe finally climaxed it left her so shattered that all she could do afterwards was lie in Maggie's arms, exhausted but happy, complete.

'Hmm,' murmured Jen. 'It's been a while.'

'Too long,' said Isa. 'We shouldn't ignore one another like we have been, I've really missed this.'

'Me too,' agreed Jen. 'I just haven't been in the mood recently.'

'I know,' said Isa. 'So I'm not complaining now.'

Jen laughed quietly and mused, 'I wonder what Chloe and Mags are doing?'

'If they've got any sense,' said Isa, 'they'll be making out like we just have.'

Jen laughed quietly again and then said in a wondering voice, 'I can't believe Chloe, makes a kill on only her third night and leads a successful hunt on her fifth.'

'She was born to be with us,' said Isa. 'Just like Caitlin was. Maggie chooses well.'

'I haven't done too badly myself,' said Jen, leaning in to take a kiss.

They lay there, naked, staring up at the stars and stretching against one another, the two of them perfectly content in the moment. Jen thought on the time that she and Isa had been together: twenty-five years was a silver anniversary and fifty was gold. What did they call it when you were together for over four hundred and seventy years? Despite that incredible length of time that she had been alive and in the world, Jen wasn't at all weary—her life of feeding and wandering suited her just fine. Being turned had simplified things for her and in an ironic way she was grateful to that beast Klaus Werlund. But she was far more grateful to Isa, who had voluntarily come over to be with her and had filled the years with the most perfect of loves.

She rolled over so that she was lying atop her partner and kissed her soundly. When they broke apart, Isa sighed, 'Don't leave it so long next time.'

'I'll try not to,' Jen promised. 'Caitlin's death affected me pretty badly.'

'It affected us all,' said Isa. 'Maggie especially although with Chloe here she'll heal pretty quickly now.'

'I'm sure she will,' said Jen. 'Come on lover, let's head back and move on.'

169

'Sure thing.'

They retrieved their clothes from where they had left them and headed back to the van; Chloe and Maggie hadn't returned yet and Jen and Isa exchanged knowing smiles.

'When shall we ditch these wheels?' Isa asked.

'Soon,' replied Jen. 'Although I quite like this little bus, there's something to be said for new vehicles.'

'I agree,' replied Isa. 'Hopefully our next one won't be a return to the noisy old monsters.'

Just then they heard laughter and saw Maggie and Chloe coming towards them. The two girls were giggling and dancing. Isa looked to Jen and said, 'Oh, to be that young again. Two hundred!' Jen just laughed and Isa continued, 'What was I doing when I was two hundred?'

'As I recall,' said Jen, 'we were coming back from Moscow.'

'Moscow!' Isa laughed. 'Whose bright idea was it to go there in winter?'

'Yours I believe,' said Jen with a big grin.

'That figures,' said Isa, rolling her eyes. 'I've never seen snow quite like that before!'

'Hip deep, wasn't it?' said Jen, still grinning.

'We ready to go?' called Maggie.

'Sure are!' replied Jen. 'Have a nice night?'

Maggie's and Chloe's smiles were answer enough. They climbed into the van and when Isa raised her eyebrows questioningly, Jen said, 'Just head east and we'll find a place to bed down when it gets close to daybreak.'

Isa smiled beatifically; Jen was her old, relaxed, carefree self and that was far more welcome than the worried, pushy woman she'd been the past couple of days, or the edgy and reticent woman she had been the last year. Isa started the van up and drove out of Mankato; a couple of hours later they were bedding down in Winona, just on the border with

170

Wisconsin, relaxed and unconcerned. They had no knowledge of Samantha Morrell.

Several hours of good, solid sleep followed by a hot, refreshing shower and a late afternoon breakfast saw Morrell and Brody as reborn. They knew their quarry was up this way, they knew it was only a matter of time before they caught Maggie and her group and put an end to them. Sam and Louise's good spirits lasted until they entered the FBI's offices in Minneapolis; they had just set themselves up at a spare desk when across the office came, 'Jesus Christ! Is that Samantha Morrell I see there, still wasting Bureau resources?'

'Fucking hell!' muttered Sam. 'I *don't* need that asshole here at this moment in time.'

'Who is he?' asked Brody in a whisper.

'Wayne Duganis,' answered Morrell. 'His daddy is well placed in DC, that's the only reason he got into the FBI.' Her tone and expression were utterly contemptuous.

Duganis strode over to where Sam and Louise were standing. Wayne was five feet, four inches tall although he affected a swagger to imply that he was closer to seven feet; he was also, well, *fat.*

'What you doin' here, Morrell?' he asked pugnaciously.

'Working,' replied Morrell shortly.

'Still on that case?'

Sam nodded.

'Jesus aitch Christ!' he exclaimed. 'If I was in charge of the Bureau I'd have fired your ass years ago!'

'Well,' said Sam, her voice dripping pure acid, 'America is dead lucky that you are not in charge otherwise the country would have gone down the crapper a long time ago.'

171

Duganis reared back as if he had been physically slapped in the face. 'You'd better watch your mouth, Morrell, otherwise . . .'

'What?' Sam barked, jutting her chin forward. 'You'll run to Pops with your thumb in your mouth, asswipe?'

Brody threw her head back and laughter peeled around the office.

Sam then noticed that standing behind Duganis, with his hand over his mouth, was Paul Jeffson. 'Hello Paul, how are you?'

'I'm well, Sam,' he replied politely. 'How are you?'

'Better than I have been,' she answered. 'Louise, meet Special Agent Jeffson, Paul, Agent Brody.'

'Good to meet you, Special Agent Jeffson,' said Louise politely.

'Likewise, Agent Brody,' Jeffson responded.

'You still haven't answered my question, Morrell,' Duganis butted in. 'What are you doin' here?'

'I did answer that question,' Sam said with a sigh. 'Do you want some blasting powder for that earwax?'

Brody's laughter peeled out again and Duganis flushed. 'Shut your mouth, weed, otherwise I'll have your badge.'

'Fuck off, asswipe!' Brody had gone from laughter to venom in the wink of an eye and Sam could see Louise's fingers twitching; she was itching to draw her gun. Duganis had that effect on people.

'How is your case progressing?' asked Jeffson, stepping in to try and defuse the situation.

Sam was about to answer but Brody interrupted with a polite, 'Do you know much about Agent Morrell's case?'

'Not that much,' admitted Jeffson.

Louise arched an eyebrow at Morrell and said, 'Well then, why don't you two gentlemen grab yourselves a seat and allow us to bring you up to speed?'

Sam grinned at her partner as she realised what Louise

was up to. She logged on to the computer on the desk and brought up her case file. Then she swivelled the monitor around so that the other two agents could see it.

'Ten years ago,' Morrell began, 'I was assigned to a case, two multiple murders, one in Ohio and the other in Indiana . . .'

'Jesus Christ!' Duganis breathed. He was reeling, Morrell had just given him all the details of her case and he couldn't believe it. 'Are you trying to tell me . . .' he began, but Morrell interrupted him.

'I'm not trying to tell you anything, Wayne,' she said. 'I am just presenting to you all the evidence I have uncovered during the ten years of this investigation. Draw your own conclusions. Brody did.' She indicated Louise. 'And then she requested to partner me.'

'But . . .' Duganis couldn't bring himself to say it. 'But . . .'

'It does explain Tacoma though,' said Jeffson quietly.

'But . . . ,' said Duganis.

'And you were finally able to kill one of them just by dragging them out into the sunlight?' Paul continued and Sam nodded affirmation.

'But . . .'

'Jesus Christ, Duganis!' Jeffson rounded on the other agent. 'Two and a half thousand rounds of ammunition did nothing to these women. Four agents and seventeen police officers died that night and they died for nothing. After the gunfight the women just slipped away.'

'But . . .' Duganis was struggling with it, trying to say it out loud. He finally managed it. 'Vampires?' His expression said louder than words that this was totally unbelievable; Jeffson's expression was similar.

'Let's put it another way then, gentlemen,' said Morrell.

173

'We have, roaming around out there, a group of women who kill people in order to drink their blood. Bullets cannot harm them but sunlight does kill them. Also, I have strong reason to believe that they have lived for at least two human lifetimes, if not longer, but still look like they're in their mid-thirties.'

There was silence for a few moments before Jeffson said, 'And there is a word to describe a creature like that.'

'Yeah,' said Duganis unhappily. 'Vampire.'

'Call them what you will,' said Sam. 'They're out there and they're not gonna stop killing. It's what they do, all they do.'

'Shit!' exclaimed Duganis. 'How long have you known this, Sam?'

'Six years,' replied Morrell.

'Why haven't you said anything before?' Wayne demanded.

'Who would believe me?' asked Sam, raising her arms up. 'It sounds crazy to my ears but that's what all the evidence I have found points to. These women are feeding.'

'And you think they're up here?' asked Jeffson.

'I have very good reason to suspect that they are either in this state or one of the neighbouring ones. They killed the night before last in Wichita, which means they'll strike again tonight. I'm praying that we can latch onto that kill quickly and track them. What I haven't had yet is a positive sighting of them from law enforcement. Once I get that then I can really pursue them.'

'How are you communicating with the locals?' asked Jeffson.

'By cellphone and e-mail,' Sam replied.

'We'll need an MCV then,' said Duganis.

'MCV?' queried Brody.

'Mobile communications vehicle,' answered Duganis. 'It

174

allows us to talk with state and local police on their radio frequencies. Makes communication a whole lot easier.'

'Hallelujah to that!' said Brody, and Duganis gave her a tight grin.

'And you really think they're up here?' Jeffson repeated.

'Pretty sure,' nodded Morrell. 'They travelled up here to get away from Chloe Lamont's home area. I'm hoping that they'll think they're far enough away and relax their guard a little.'

'That's a lot of hoping, Sam,' Jeffson pointed out.

'Hope's all I've had for the last six years,' Sam replied quietly.

Duganis stood up then and said, 'I'll arrange the MCV; Sam, you inform all the locals up here that we'll be contactable via their radios.'

'Will do,' replied Sam, her eyes widening in surprise as Duganis turned and strode purposefully out of the office.

'He changed his tune rather quickly,' noted Brody.

'He's had all the wind taken out of his sails, that's why,' said Jeffson. 'I have too.'

'Are you with me on this, Paul?' Sam asked in a quiet voice.

'I have to be, Sam,' replied Jeffson sadly. 'I survived Tacoma but I blamed you for that fiasco.' His face became mortified. 'But how were you supposed to know?'

'How was anyone supposed to know?' Morrell countered. 'I didn't discover the truth about these women until two years after Tacoma.'

'And you've carried it on your own ever since?' Jeffson was full of admiration.

'Someone had to,' replied Morrell. 'Otherwise these women will be unopposed.' She paused a moment and reflected, then said, 'But with Louise here and you and Duganis we might just stand a chance of stopping them.'

'Might do,' agreed Jeffson. 'But there is a problem.'

'What?' asked Sam.

'If you try and request any more agents to help with this case then that request will be denied.'

'What?' Sam sat bolt upright in her chair.

'Management has finally tired of your inability to resolve this case. Notice came here from DC about ten minutes before you arrived,' Paul informed her, wearing a sad expression.

'Fuckers!' snarled Morrell. 'Are they going to prevent me from utilising the locals as well?'

'No,' replied Jeffson, shaking his head. 'You still have that at the moment.'

'Fine!' said Morrell, slumping back in her seat and folding her arms across her chest. 'I'll do this without the Bureau then.'

'Probably better that way,' said Jeffson. 'Other agents on this and we could easily lose these girls.'

'Not this time, Paul.' Morrell's voice was cast iron.

Chapter 15

Rachael sat in the car, breathless and exhilarated. Why? She didn't know. She had been asleep when her dreams turned into a sensation of hurtling through darkness. She sat in the driver's seat, on the cusp between wakefulness and sleep, and felt herself flying. And that taste in her mouth, what was that?

She had left Des Moines around mid-morning and headed in a general northerly direction although she didn't rush. She had the tuner earpiece in and was listening in to the police chatter all the way but she heard nothing about 'Chloe's group'. When she reached Waterloo, a hundred or so miles northeast of Des Moines, she realised she was moving away from her sister again and so changed direction to head directly north. She arrived in Rochester, Minnesota during the late afternoon and stopped. Chloe was still asleep and Rachael could only feel that her sister was near but had no idea which way to go. She grabbed herself some dinner at another roadside diner and was surprised at the high quality of food she was served; it certainly tasted good. As a result of a rather full belly she had fallen asleep in the car only to be woken just after nightfall by the strange rushing sensation. Was it something to do with Chloe?

She could sense that her sister was somewhat west of her, but how far? Rachael didn't know and so stayed where she was. Some time around midnight she fell asleep again and

177

didn't awaken until some time after sunrise. She could feel that Chloe was now somewhere slightly east of her and so she left Rochester and headed for La Crosse, a town that lay just the other side of the state line in Wisconsin, on the banks of the Mississippi. When she got there she sensed her sister was somewhere west of her again. This didn't frustrate Rachael, not yet anyway—she was staying in touch with Chloe and that was enough for the moment. If she found that the police were closing in, though, then she'd try and home right in.

With Jeffson and Duganis with her on the case, Morrell was able to hit home to every police department the urgency of detecting these women. Missing persons, that was the key. If four or more people had gone missing during the night then she wanted to know about it and quickly. One piece of luck that was on Sam's side was that the girls didn't really go into very large towns, let alone cities. These girls much preferred the countryside and that meant that detecting them through missing persons became that little bit easier.

After arranging for an MCV, Duganis and Jeffson had gone to bed in order to be awake to take over from Morrell and Brody. Sam and Louise were now on the nightshift proper and this meant twenty-four-hour coverage, with Paul and Wayne monitoring during the day.

It was during 'shift change' that morning that they got a call.

'Special Agent Morrell,' Sam answered her cellphone.

'Good morning, Agent Morrell,' said the caller. 'I'm John Aysebury, the sheriff here in Mankato, southern Minnesota.'

'How can I help you, Sheriff?' Sam asked.

'Last night we received notification from the FBI,' began Aysebury, 'that a group of wanted criminals could very well be in the area and you wanted to hear from any police department that had four or more missing persons in a night.'

'That is correct, Sheriff,' said Morrell.

'Well, four teenagers drove out last night to a local beauty spot called Paulson Lake and they didn't make it home. I've had four sets of parents down here first thing this morning raising hell,' said Aysebury. 'I'm up at the spot now and a cursory inspection shows me a set of fresh tyre tracks entering the site but none leaving. Furthermore, there are four patches of blood in the grass here and they look fresh.'

Could it be? Sam prayed. Was she right behind them?

'Sheriff,' began Morrell, 'have some of your officers move around the town asking anyone who was up late last night if they saw a Roadtrek Versatile in the area.'

'Already ahead of you there on that one, Agent Morrell,' said Aysebury. 'When the kids were reported missing I acted on your notice and despatched officers to find out whether or not your four women were seen here. The women weren't but we do have a witness who claims to have seen a motor home leaving the town in the early hours of this morning. It was headed eastward.'

'That could very well be them,' said Morrell. 'Have you found the car the teenagers were in yet?'

'No, we haven't,' replied Aysebury. 'And we've searched all around the lake.'

'I'm getting a horrible feeling that the women I'm chasing were in your town last night. Pray I'm wrong, but when you find the car you may very well find four dead bodies in it.'

'But where's the car?' asked Aysebury. 'I've got tyre tracks leading in but none leaving.'

'Try the lake,' suggested Morrell quietly.

'Aw shit!' exclaimed Aysebury. 'Okay, I'll get a couple of divers to search the lake and I'll contact you the soonest I know anything.'

179

'Speak to you then, Sheriff,' said Morrell and the connection was cut.

'Possible lead?' enquired Brody. Sam noticed that her partner was by her side constantly now and this comforted her greatly.

'Yes,' replied Morrell. 'Four kids didn't make it home last night.' And she repeated what John Aysebury had told her.

Jeffson and Duganis were listening as well and when she finished Wayne asked, 'Do you want to head out east now?'

Sam thought a few moments before replying, 'Let's leave it a couple of hours and see if Mankato get back to us with any more news. If we don't hear anything by midday we'll decide then.'

Jeffson nodded and said to the two women, 'Okay, you girls go and get some sleep. If we hear anything we'll wake you.'

Sam and Louise headed out of the office, Morrell handing her cellphone to Jeffson. When they were gone, Duganis asked Paul, 'What do you make of all this, bullshit or what?'

'Or what,' replied Jeffson.

'Yeah,' said Duganis in a depressed tone. 'Me too. I wish I could call it all bullshit but the evidence is pretty compelling.'

' "Not murdering, feeding",' Jeffson murmured.

'Jesus! That makes it worse,' said Duganis. 'Come on, let's make ourselves useful and see if we can spot that Roadtrek. They put tinfoil on the windshield?'

Jeffson nodded and the two men got to work.

Morrell and Brody entered the office just after midday to find both Jeffson and Duganis on the phone. Wayne finished his call first and said to Sam, 'A couple of things.

We've tried to see if we could locate the Roadtrek but so far, zip.'

'I'd be surprised if you could find it,' said Sam. 'They seem to have this uncanny ability for moving around unnoticed but thanks for trying anyway.'

'That's okay,' said Duganis. 'We had confirmation earlier that the Roadtrek was heading east. Owatonna sheriff's office contacted us to say that a Roadtrek Versatile with Oklahoma plates pulled up at a gas station just outside the town. However, they didn't fill right up, they only bought ten bucks' worth of gas.'

'Which means that they'll be changing vehicles real soon,' said Sam immediately.

'Yeah, that was my guess too.'

'Any word from Mankato?' she asked.

'None yet,' replied Duganis. 'But Paul might be speaking to them right now. One last bit though, the police in La Crosse, Wisconsin reported seeing Ruth Lamont's station wagon there today.' He looked a bit puzzled by this.

'Shit,' said Sam quietly. 'Chloe Lamont's twin sister, Rachael, is driving that. She seems to have an ability to track Chloe and her being here means that we are definitely close to them. But I don't want her diving in the middle of this at the wrong moment.'

'Why not have her apprehended and sent home then?' asked Duganis.

'Not until we get a positive sighting of these girls our-selves. Rachael's ability to track Chloe is a general indicator of where they are. Until we get a confirmed sighting I'll leave Rachael where she is.'

Duganis nodded understanding.

Paul ended his telephone call and immediately walked over to where Sam was.

'Mankato just called back,' he began. 'They found the

car in the lake some twenty feet from the bank. The bodies of the four missing teenagers were inside.' Paul went silent a moment before adding, 'The sheriff says that all four had their throats savaged.'

'That, people,' said Morrell, 'was a group hunt. They haven't done one of those for a year now. They used to do them all the time but I think my killing Caitlin Baker made them more cautious.' She then turned bleak eyes on Brody and said, 'Chloe Lamont's definitely one of them now.'

Louise nodded sombrely.

'What do you want to do, Sam?' asked Wayne.

'Let's get on the road. They fed in the south of the state and we've had two sightings of the vehicle headed east.' Sam looked at the map and continued, 'They won't kill tonight so they could put some real distance between Mankato and their next kills.' She looked at her three fellow agents and said, 'I'm gonna take a risk and try and get ahead of them. Let's get to . . .' Sam studied the map and finished with, 'Rockford, Illinois.'

The other three nodded and with that they all left the office.

Rachael stayed in La Crosse and waited for Chloe to move. She had a moment of real panic when a police patrol car slowly cruised past her, the officer inside giving her car very close scrutiny. However, the patrol car moved on and Rachael was left in peace.

In the afternoon the police-radio traffic information got very busy and Rachael learned that she was close to her sister. Four teenagers had been found dead in Mankato in neighbouring Minnesota. Rachael wept a few tears on hearing this; it brought it home to her just how much Chloe had changed. She also heard that all law enforcement in Wisconsin was on full alert for the group as they were last seen heading east in a motor home and could very well be in the state. As the sun was beginning to set she heard that Morrell was situated in Rockford, Illinois and Rachael knew that the agent was trying to get ahead of the group. Rachael realised that she would have to get to Chloe tonight if she was ever to stand a chance of saying goodbye to her sister. Morrell was moving in for the kill and the group's time was fast running out.

Shortly after sundown Rachael felt her sister on the move again and so waited a little while before setting off herself. Her intention was to intercept them, warn them and maybe, just maybe save her sister. She ended up in Baraboo.

She missed them by just one town.

Sundown and the group was up and about, laughing and joking and in no hurry to get anywhere.

'What we doin' tonight, Jen?' Maggie asked with bright eyes. Being this far north of New Mexico had released a lot of tension that Maggie was unaware she'd had.

'Let's find a bar or diner,' replied Jen. 'Shoot the breeze or some such for a couple of hours. We've got no place we need to be in a hurry so . . .' She waved her hand in an offhand manner.

Chloe smiled broadly as she was finally seeing her sisters as they had been for countless decades. Gone was the tense, nervous edginess that she had first seen in them, caused initially by Caitlin's death a year ago and compounded by her own abduction.

'Can we visit Chicago?' she asked the others.

'Why do you want to go there?' Isa asked her.

'Dunno,' replied Chloe. 'I've just never been there before and seein' as we're up this way, well . . .' She didn't bother finishing.

'We can always feed there tomorrow night,' suggested

Maggie. 'It's a big city so there's plenty of people . . .' She left it hanging.

'Why not?' Jen smiled with a shrug of her shoulders. 'We tend not to visit cities so it might make a nice change.' Jen looked thoughtful for a few moments before adding, 'We haven't been to Chicago for nearly a hundred years.'

'It's been that long?' Isa looked surprised by this.

'You're right, Jen,' said Maggie, her eyes wide. 'Last time we were there Caitlin was still on my wrist. Man!' She shook her head. 'Where does time go?'

'Behind us,' said Jen with a smile. 'Which isn't too much of a problem as we've still got plenty ahead of us.'

Isa smiled and said, 'Sure we have. But let's put it to good use, shall we?'

All four laughed in agreement, and as they drove out of Winona Isa commented that Chicago would be a good place to get another vehicle. A quiet vehicle.

They never reached the windy city. Two hours later and they were pulling up in the Wisconsin town of Reedsburg. There they found a diner, ordered some drinks and light snacks and just sat there, idly talking for a couple of hours.

Chapter 16

'Sheriff Pullman, you there, Sir?'

'Yah, who's this?'

'Patrolman Deekes, Sir.'

'What's up, Weylan?'

'Well, Sir, you know that FBI notice we received last night?'

'Yah.'

'Well, I'm looking into Lou's diner this very moment and I swear that in there I can see Maggie O'Hearn and Chloe Lamont. They're with two others but I can't quite make them out.'

'Weylan, I'm not in the mood for games.'

'I'm not playing, Sir! Not on something like this. I'm looking at the printouts and I'm looking at these women and I'd swear that it was Maggie O'Hearn and Chloe Lamont I'm seeing. I think you'd better come out and check, Sir, just in case my eyes are deceiving me.'

'They probably are but you stay right where you are and I'll come and have a look.'

'Thank you, Sir.'

'Look in there, Sir,' said Deekes, pointing to the diner's windows some five minutes after calling his boss. 'I'm almost positive that's them!'

'Calmly Weylan,' said Pullman in a low rumble. Sheriff Pullman *always* spoke in a low rumble. He looked into the diner and saw the women that Deekes was referring to. He then looked at the printouts he and every other officer had of the FBI's notice. He looked at the women again. 'Shit Weylan!' He breathed. 'You're absolutely right. It *is* them!'

'We gonna call the FBI?' asked Deekes.

'Shit no!' spat the sheriff. 'These felons are on my turf, therefore it's my job to bring them in. You stay here, I'm gonna call reinforcements.' And with that he turned and quickly walked back to his patrol car.

Sheriff Tyler Pullman had been Reedsburg's senior law officer for over two decades. He prided himself on the town's incredibly low crime record, a result of his zero-tolerance attitude toward crime. His motto was:

'Crack down hard on the petty crime and the really big stuff will leave you alone.'

And it worked. Theft, burglary, fist fights, you name it, it hardly ever happened here. As for drug dealing, rape and all the other heavy crimes? Forget it! They *never* happened here.

Four criminals wanted by the FBI, moving freely in his town? No way!

Chloe was surprised and rather disappointed at her first food and drink after being turned. It had some taste to it but nothing like what she clearly remembered.

'We don't need to eat and drink,' Maggie had reminded her. 'We just do it to blend in.'

The last couple of hours had been spent reminiscing about past exploits and places that they had seen. Chloe loved hearing all these stories from decades gone by but she did feel a bit left out as she didn't really have any stories of her own. Nevertheless, Maggie, Jen and Isa asked her questions about her hometown and childhood and very soon she was joining in with the conversation. They were surprised and a little upset to learn that Chloe had a twin.

'Do you miss her?' Isa had asked.

'No, I don't,' replied Chloe in a quiet voice. 'And I find that really strange as we were inseparable most of the time.'

'Being turned has had some effect, I'd imagine,' ventured Jen. 'Remember, you're not entirely human anymore.'

Chloe had nodded understanding although she looked rather sad.

They moved on to other topics of conversation, other times in the past.

'Do you remember what Caitlin always wanted to do?' Maggie asked in a conspiratorially low voice, her eyes glowing bright and her lips split into a beaming smile.

'Yeah!' Jen and Isa said in unison, nodding and trying hard to control their laughter.

Maggie then turned to Chloe and said, 'Just like Jen couldn't deny Isa anything, so it was with me and Caitlin. However . . .'

More stifled chortling from Jen and Isa.

'There was one thing she always wanted to do but none of us would let her.'

'What was that?' asked Chloe quietly, a smile on her lips.

'She always wanted to climb aboard a Greyhound and say . . .' Maggie's face brightened even more, ' "*Listen up everybody, no one's gettin' off this bus alive!*" And then kill all the passengers.'

Jen, Isa and Maggie had tears streaming down their faces and it took them a minute or two to get themselves under control. Finally Jen was able to say, 'There was no way we were ever going to do that! Too high profile and totally unnecessary.' She pondered a moment and then added, 'Probably a lot of fun though.'

'That was Caitlin all over,' said Maggie, wiping her eyes.

187

'She had a real wild streak in her, her motto was simply "have fun".'

'Sure was,' said Jen. 'I really miss her.'

'We all do,' said Isa, and Chloe could see the bittersweet cast to Maggie's eyes. Maggie would always hurt for Caitlin but she was over the worst of it now.

'Listen up,' said Isa quietly across the table. 'As much as I'm enjoying this evening—the first such evening we've had in over a year—if we wanna hit Chicago by sunrise then I think we'd best get moving now.'

'Good idea,' agreed Jen. 'Ladies, shall we?'

Maggie, Jen and Isa picked up their bags and all four of them made their way out of the door.

As soon as they were outside they were suddenly bathed in bright, white light.

'THIS IS THE POLICE!' said a voice through a loud hailer. 'LIE DOWN ON THE FLOOR WITH YOUR HANDS BEHIND YOUR HEAD. YOU ARE COMPLETELY SURROUNDED!'

They were too. Tyler Pullman *never* bullshitted. He had been sheriff in this town for over twenty years and knew all the fine, upstanding citizens it contained. More importantly, he knew all the fine, upstanding citizens who had firearms and knew how to use them properly. When Pullman said he was getting reinforcements he wasn't joking. Not only was the entire sheriff's department, apart from the dispatcher, there but also numerous townsfolk who had been formed into an armed militia. There was a ring of police and civilian cars around the diner's entrance, forming a cordon, and when Pullman had finished hailing the quartet there was the sound of many guns being cocked and primed for firing.

'I REPEAT, THIS IS THE POLICE!' Tyler's voice boomed again. 'LIE DOWN ON THE FLOOR WITH YOUR HANDS

188

BEHIND YOUR HEAD. YOU ARE COMPLETELY SUR-ROUNDED! THIS IS YOUR FINAL WARNING!'

Jen's acute eyesight pierced through the glare of spot-lights to see what lay behind. Numerous guns, all pointing at them.

'Girls,' she said to the other three, 'we're gonna have to shoot our way out of this one.'

'Ahh fuck!' exclaimed Isa quietly. 'This is gonna be Tacoma all over again.'

'No help for it,' said Jen. 'We're gonna have to blast our way out of this and then get the hell out of here.'

'Okay,' said Maggie. 'Three.'

'Two,' said Isa.

'GO!' barked Jen.

Suddenly Maggie, Jen and Isa literally exploded into rapid motion. In one graceful, fluid move Jen pulled her gun out of her coat, flipped the safety catch off and cocked it whilst performing a high forward somersault. She landed on the hood of a patrol car so hard that she busted the car's suspension *and* pushed the engine off its mountings. As the car's front end dipped down and the engine block thunked to the ground Jen fired off a shot; the bullet took Pullman straight through the forehead. She then leapt from the hood and over the car's roof to land behind the line of shooters and began pumping lead into them.

While Jen was somersaulting, Isa sprang backwards and ran diagonally to the right up the diner's wall before launching herself off it to land catlike on the other side of the police line. Like Jen, she too had pulled out her gun in mid-air and primed it so as soon as she landed she was shooting the police and town militia.

Maggie leapt upwards and to the left and planted a foot on a nearby lamppost. Then she sprang upwards and twisted to plant the same foot on the diner's wall and, like Isa, propelled herself through the air to land on the other side of the police line. Like her two sisters she had also pulled out her gun, flipped the safety catch off and cocked it in mid-air. As soon as she landed, she too was firing bullets into the police.

Chloe hadn't had chance to learn how to shoot her gun properly but she pulled it out anyway, flipped off the safety catch and cocked it. Holding her gun in both hands she stood still, took careful aim and then began squeezing off shots one at a time.

The three women had moved *so* quickly, so *impossibly*, that there was a frozen pause in the police before they were able to react. Practically everybody just stood there open-mouthed as the three women did things no ordinary person could do. When they finally did react it was more like panic fire; bullets went winging in all directions, some ploughed through the diner's windows to hit the patrons within, others flew harmlessly into the sky. Those members of the militia who were not directly attacked took time to pick their targets and began shooting with more accuracy. But it did them no good; these girls were impervious to guns and when these shooters saw their bullets having no effect panic began to set in among them.

Jen and Isa were right in the thick of it, leaping up and over the heads of the militia like tigers to land in among them, causing even more panic. When their guns ran out of ammunition they didn't bother to reload, they just set in with their teeth and fingernails, ripping and tearing neck flesh. Maggie too didn't bother to reload when her gun ran dry; her knife sliced out again and again with deadly accuracy. Chloe, standing still, was an easier target for the shooters and she took numerous bullet hits all over her body. But she stayed calm and picked her targets carefully. She was a rather inaccurate shot but still pretty good for a first-timer; when she ran out of ammunition she carefully

190

reloaded whilst taking a few steps forward. Still taking bullet hits she stood firm and began squeezing off shots again.

In taking these girls on all the police and townsfolk did was ensure that they fell before the reaper's scythe. The scene in front of Lou's diner resembled carnage. Twenty-four police and militiamen had surrounded the front of the diner and six minutes later, when the gunfight ended, only one survived. That survivor was Patrolman Weylan Deekes; he only lived because when he saw his bullets having no effect on these women he just lay down on the floor and played dead. Some people would have said that it was a cowardly thing to do, but it saved his life.

'*Merde!*' snarled Jen in her native French. Her mouth and fingers were smeared with blood and this, combined with her expression, would have caused the stoutest heart to quail. She surveyed the scene before her: dead bodies and spent bullet casings littered the street. 'Let's get out of here!'

They picked up their bags and ran down a side street.

'My God!' said Isa. 'They must have put Chloe's picture out nationwide. And there's us thinking we were safe in the north.'

'It gets worse though, doesn't it?' said Maggie. 'Two Tacomas in eight years? The police are gonna put two and two together, not to mention the FBI.'

'No shit!' exclaimed Jen. 'Let's find a vehicle and get away from here.'

They all paused in the shadows for a moment and tensed up. There was the quiet chinking sound of metal hitting concrete as they expelled the bullets from their bodies. Then they were moving again.

'You thinkin' what I'm thinkin'?' Isa asked her partner.

'Yeah,' said Jen. 'Mexico, for at least a couple of decades.'

'Why not Canada?' asked Chloe. 'It's a hell of a lot closer.'

'Because our feeding gets noticed real easy up there,'

191

replied Maggie. 'After Tacoma we went up there and it was the most uncomfortable eighteen months we had ever spent. The police were all over our back trail and we nearly got caught a couple of times. Jen's right, we've gotta go to Mexico although I can't speak the lingo.'

Chloe rattled off a string of Spanish.

'In that case you can order the beer then,' said Maggie, grinning.

'Potential wheels!' said Isa, running over to a panel van, a Dodge Caravan. She quickly toured around it before saying, 'No alarm on it.'

Jen and Maggie quickly scanned the area with their senses and felt no one watching.

'Let's take it,' said Jen.

Isa fished her coat hanger out of the bag she was carrying and had the vehicle open within ten seconds. Within thirty seconds all four of them were inside and the engine was fired up. They left the town quickly but not so quick as to draw attention. As soon as they were out of town Isa put her foot to the floor.

'Stay off the main highways,' Jen said.

'It'll take longer to get to the border,' Isa pointed out.

'Yeah, but the cops are gonna be all out looking for us real soon so stick to the back roads,' said Jen, looking at the road map.

'Not just the cops either,' said Maggie. 'The FBI will come in on this one.'

'I know,' replied Jen. 'That's why we should stay away from major routes. The authorities are gonna be watching them very carefully.' She perused the map again. 'Christ!' she spat. 'We did *not* need that little episode!'

'Do you think someone's onto us, Jen?' Maggie asked. 'I mean, they were waiting for us and in numbers. All that for an abduction?'

'I don't think so,' replied Jen. 'I think Isa's right, they

put Chloe's picture out nationwide. Veer west into Iowa as soon as you can,' she told Isa.

'Sure thing,' replied Isa.

Jen turned back to Maggie and said, 'I mean, who knows about us three?'

Maggie and Isa shrugged their shoulders. None of them knew about Samantha Morrell.

The Dodge Caravan roared south into the night.

'Calling FBI Special Agent Samantha Morrell, come in please!'

The call came in over the radio and the voice sounded fairly young and very upset. Morrell was sitting in the back of the MCV with Louise. Duganis and Jeffson were up the front; Paul was in the driver's seat. The MCV was parked outside Rockford's main police station, fully gassed and ready to go.

Sam picked up the radio handset and responded, 'This is Special Agent Morrell, who am I speaking to?'

'This is Patrolman Weylan Deekes, I'm with the Reedsburg sheriff's department,' replied the caller. 'Reedsburg's in Wisconsin, Ma'am, some seventy miles northwest of Madison,' he added.

'Got it!' said Brody, looking at a map.

'What's up?' Sam asked him. There was a sinking feeling in her stomach.

'Oh God!' he exclaimed. 'It's awful, just plain awful.'

'Talk to me, Patrolman.' Sam put steel in her voice. 'Tell me what's happened.'

'Well, Ma'am,' began Deekes, 'I was just touring the town when I thought I saw one of the women on your notice in our local diner. I took a closer look, careful mind, and sure enough, it was Maggie O'Hearn. Sittin' next to her was Chloe Lamont too, so I contacted the sheriff and he came out and looked. He agreed it was them and so got the rest of the department plus some townsfolk and made to arrest them as they were coming out of the diner.'

Sam closed her eyes and bowed her head when she heard this. She pretty much knew what the patrolman was going to say next.

'When they were out in the open Sheriff Pullman loud-hailed them and told them to surrender. But they didn't and that's when the shootin' started.' He choked back a sob and said, 'Our guns did nothin' to them, nothin'. There were nearly thirty of us started out and now I'm the only one left.'

Sam just sat there with her head bowed; her last chance to finish these girls had just been blown.

'Ma'am, are you still there?' asked Deekes.

Seeing that Sam wasn't going to reply, Louise took up the handset and said 'Patrolman Deekes, this is Agent Brody, can you hold a moment?'

'Sure thing, Agent Brody, apart from the dispatcher I'm all that's left of the sheriff's office here.'

Brody turned to her partner. 'Sam?'

'That's it,' said Sam in a defeated voice. 'They'll run for cover now, straight over the border into Canada.'

'No they won't!' Brody shot back sternly.

Morrell raised her head, her eyes showing utter defeat. 'Louise, Canada's a huge country. They'll disappear up there.'

'No they won't,' Brody said again. 'Yeah, Canada's a big country, second biggest in the world in fact. But its population's only thirty million; America has two hundred and sixty million.' She then waited for Morrell to take in what she had just said.

Morrell remained confused for a couple of moments before realisation dawned on her. 'Their feeding gets noticed up there!' she said.

194

'It sure does!' said Brody. 'I checked the Canadian police files for the eighteen months after Tacoma and there was a *marked* increase in the number of killings up there. These girls show up north of the border as Canada has far, far fewer homicides than we do.'

'But they won't stay in America, they'll . . .'

'Exactly!' interrupted Brody. 'They'll head for the border, yes—the *Mexican* border! They've got to traverse practically the whole of the United States to get there though. We can still catch them!'

Morrell swung into action again and got on the radio.

'Patrolman Deekes?'

'Yes, Ma'am?'

'Your priority task at this moment is to find what vehicle those four left your town in. They were planning to switch vehicles soon anyway and what has just occurred means they'll do it now. Tour the town, knock on every door and find out what vehicle has been stolen since the gunfight. It'll probably be a van but it could be anything smaller than a truck.'

'But I'm the only police officer here,' Deekes protested.

'Don't worry about that, I'll contact the state police and get them to send some troopers down to help you. Your focus is to find the vehicle they left town in. You got that?'

'Sure thing, Ma'am!' Deekes replied, his voice conveying the backbone he had just discovered.

'Get to it.' And Sam then immediately set about contacting the Wisconsin state police.

While she was doing that Brody began alerting state patrols all the way down to the southern border, from coast to coast. She assumed that the group would take the most direct and quickest route to Mexico but she wanted to make sure that *everybody* was on the lookout for them.

Duganis and Jeffson had heard the whole conversation and as Morrell and Brody began galvanising the police to the south Paul started the van up and began heading in that direction as well.

The chase was on.

They roared on through the night, Isa keeping the Dodge van between seventy-five and a hundred. They stopped at a gas station in Marion, Iowa to fill the vehicle up. Despite having taken numerous bullet hits by the time they had reached Marion the wounds had healed up, such was their regenerative power, and they only looked like they'd been in a fist fight. As the attendant filled the vehicle up he commented on Isa's reddened face.

'Violent boyfriend,' she had replied. 'Why do you think I'm filling this thing right up? I intend to get as far away from him as possible.'

'Wise move, lady,' the attendant said and then said no more except, 'Thanks!' when Isa told him to keep the change.

'Crack open a beer for me and toast my freedom,' she said.

'Will do!'

They carried on, steering clear of the highways and major interstates and sticking to the more rural roads. This meant that Isa had to slow down a little, but only a little.

They left it to the last possible moment to darken the vehicle and Isa kept on driving well past dawn. They finally came to rest in the town of Carthage, which lay in the southwestern corner of Missouri. Despite having put about five hundred miles between them and the gunfight, Chloe could clearly see that Jen was extremely worried. As they bedded down that morning Chloe realised that her sisters were really afraid, but that didn't stop any of them falling asleep straight away.

Chapter 17

The MCV headed south all night. When Jeffson was driving Duganis took the opportunity to sleep, and as soon as Jeffson began to nod off at the wheel during the early hours Wayne awoke and the van briefly halted while the drivers changed.

Forty minutes into their southward journey, Patrolman Deekes contacted them again. He reported that a Dodge Caravan had been stolen from the town; he gave them the licence plate. That information went out to *all* police forces to the south.

Jeffson and Duganis had kept the MCV to a sedate sixty-five all the way down—sedate compared with Isa's speed. However, they were travelling along the interstates so they covered some miles, and at seven-twenty that morning they were approaching Springfield in southern Missouri.

That's when the call came in.

'Special Agent Morrell? This is the Missouri state patrol.'

'Go ahead, state patrol,' replied Sam.

'We've just received a call from the sheriff's office in Carthage that a Dodge Caravan bearing Wisconsin plates was seen entering the town at about seven o'clock this morning.'

'Thank you very much, state patrol,' said Sam, her face breaking into a near smile as she saw that Carthage was very close to them. 'We are just approaching Springfield and so we'll be there within the hour.'

'Would you like our assistance?' asked the state patrol.

'Very much,' replied Morrell. 'However, no sirens.'

'Understood, Ma'am, we'll despatch several units to aid you. Furthermore, Carthage sheriff's office is awaiting your arrival, but the department will not act unless ordered by you.'

'Thank you very much.' And Sam breathed a huge sigh of relief at this last.

Duganis was driving when the call came in and he put his foot down. They arrived in Carthage thirty minutes later. When they entered the town they saw a state-patrol vehicle waiting for them and the driver waved his arm, indicating that they should follow him. They were led to the other side of town where a number of warehouses were situated, but there they were forced to pull up and get out; the sheriff's office had cordoned off several streets.

'Special Agent Morrell? I'm Sheriff Baylock,' said a man wearing a Kevlar vest and riot helmet and toting a pump-action shotgun.

'Glad to meet you, Sheriff,' said Sam, shaking his hand. She introduced Brody, Jeffson and Duganis.

'One of my officers saw the Dodge enter the town and followed them here,' said Baylock. 'The vehicle entered that storage shed over there.' And he pointed to a small wooden building sandwiched between two much larger structures about halfway down the street. 'As soon as he saw them pull up he reported it in and we then set about sealing this area off. As far as we can ascertain, the occupants of the vehicle are still there.'

'Excellent work, Sheriff,' Morrell congratulated him. 'The first thing we have to do is confirm that the felons we are pursuing are in that vehicle. Do you have any spare Kevlar?'

'We sure do,' replied the sheriff and led them over to a

198

van. Sam, Louise, Paul and Wayne donned the bullet-proof armour along with riot helmets.

'Okay,' said Sam. 'Just us five will enter that building, but quietly.' And she looked at each of the four in turn, emphasising her point. With that she turned and began walking towards the storage shed, the others following.

When she reached the entrance she peered in. The interior was gloomy but there was more than enough light for her to see clearly. Her heart leapt—the Dodge's rear screen was covered by tinfoil. Slowly and carefully she entered the shed, making sure that each footstep was placed carefully to minimise noise. She glanced behind her and saw the others doing the same. Morrell's pulse rate increased. All the Caravan's windows had been covered, as had the windshield, save a dark strip running across at driver's eye level. Standing just ahead of the driver's door, Sam took a deep breath and then bent her head to the strip in the windshield and peered in.

The interior of the vehicle was very dark and it took several moments for Sam's eyesight to adjust to the severe gloom. Finally she was able to make out details of the interior: the front seats on which were a holdall and two knapsacks; behind the seats, into the rear of the vehicle, it was even darker, but up near the rear doors Sam could see two pairs of feet. She walked around the front of the van and peered in from the passenger's side, and there she could make out another two pairs of feet at the back.

There were four people asleep in this van. Four girls. Her girls.

She looked to the other four, who were all regarding her with extreme agitation; she signalled that they should exit the shed.

Outside, Sam took a deep breath.

'It's them, isn't it?' asked Brody. Her face couldn't hide the excitement she felt.

'I can't be one-hundred-percent sure,' replied Morrell, 'but the windows are all covered and there are four people asleep in the back.' She looked at Brody and said, 'My gut tells me it's them.'

'How do you want to proceed, Agent Morrell?' asked Baylock.

'With extreme caution,' replied Sam. 'They are asleep and will remain so until nightfall unless we wake them. Therefore we must act as quietly as possible.' She walked out into the middle of the road and surveyed the area.

'Okay,' she said, walking slowly along the street. 'The thing we need to do is wheel that van out into the street. Point the back doors towards the sun and then open them up.'

'Why?' asked Baylock.

'Because it's the only way I know to kill them,' replied Sam. When she saw the puzzlement on the sheriff's face and the questions that were starting to form she added, 'Please trust me on this, Sheriff.'

Baylock looked to the other agents, who only nodded. Baylock nodded, although Sam could see that he couldn't understand why.

'The first thing we have to do,' began Sam, 'is disable that van's engine so that if they do wake up they can't just drive off.'

'That's simple,' said Baylock. 'Just pop the hood and disconnect the battery.'

'Can that be done quietly?' asked Morrell.

'Sure,' replied Baylock after a moment's consideration. 'Won't be dead silent, mind, but we can do that without waking those inside.'

'Okay, cutting the hand-brake cable should be fairly simple,' Sam stated and this was met by nods from the men. 'Steering the vehicle from outside though, how do we go about that?'

'Why do we need to steer the vehicle, Sam?' asked Jeffson.

'Because I want to wheel that vehicle right out into the open before we wrench those rear doors apart,' replied Sam. 'The moment sunlight hits them they are going to wake up and *move*.' She pointed to the end of the street and said, 'Right about there.'

The street ended as a 'T'—you could only turn left or right; straight ahead and you were onto a large patch of open wasteland. Moreover, there were no buildings on either corner—the area was completely open.

'Good killing ground,' Brody commented.

'Let's hope,' replied Morrell quietly. She turned to the others and said, 'We're only going to get the one shot at this so let's plan it carefully.'

The next couple of hours saw activity that was strange in that it was carried out almost silently. State troopers had moved into the town to bolster the sheriff's department and two rings of police were thrown around the area of the storage shed. The first ring surrounded the immediate area; all personnel wore Kevlar armour and everyone save the federal agents carried pump-action shotguns. The second ring was further out; the personnel were armed with high-powered rifles. They were there just in case the girls some-how managed to break out through the first ring; Morrell was taking no chances. She knew that guns wouldn't actually harm the girls but shotguns do pack a hell of a punch, enough to knock them over, slow them right down. And if they did manage to break out of the inner ring then the outer ring's rifles would turn the vehicle they were in into Swiss cheese. Sam's aim with both rings of police was the same—keep the girls in the sunlight.

Once all the police were in position Morrell and her colleagues, together with Sheriff Baylock and another offi-cer, once more moved into the storage shed. Very gently, Jeffson and the officer released the catch on the hood, and

201

there was a metallic *thock* as the lid popped up. Everyone's hearts jumped into their mouths and pulse rates went through the ceiling.

But there was no movement from within the van.

Duganis crept forward and quickly removed the leads from the battery; the vehicle would not start now. Jeffson lowered the hood so that it was sitting just above its normal closed position and the officer took out a pair of heavy-duty clippers, then he crawled under the vehicle. *Twang!*

Hearts in mouths again.

Still no movement from within. Once they had calmed themselves they set about the job of being able to steer the vehicle from outside. The solution was fairly simple: attach a bar to the steering rack. But doing this with the absolute minimum of noise made the task tense and nerve wracking. Every knock and metallic *clang* resulted in everybody freezing and all eyes going to the rear of the vehicle. Sam looked at Baylock and saw that he was very red in the face; too much more of this and he could very well have a stroke.

Sam had told them that if they had to speak then to put their mouth close to the person's ear and use the quietest whisper. Sam put her mouth close to Baylock's ear and said, 'Sheriff, you better go outside, you don't look very well.'

The look of pathetic gratitude on his face made her feel sorry for him. He put his mouth near her ear and whispered, 'I'm sorry, Agent Morrell, but I've got fairly high blood pressure and this situation is not good for me.'

'Then go outside and double check that everything's in position,' Sam told him.

'I'll send one of my boys in to help you push the van out.' And with that he crept out of the shed.

The replacement was the deputy sheriff and he stood at the entrance to the shed waiting to be called upon. Sam left him there. Finally the bar was attached and Jeffson gave her the thumbs up; she beckoned the deputy over and all six of them went to the front of the van. Louise manned the steering bar and the others bent their backs and pushed.

Ever so slowly they manoeuvred the vehicle out of the shed; Louise hauled on the bar and the Caravan slowly turned to the right. Once it was pointing down the street, Louise pulled the bar back into a central position. It was nearly midday now and the sun shone down from a clear blue sky. Dressed up in Kevlar body armour and riot helmets, the six people pushing the van began to sweat. Sam was struck by the almost deathly silence—this was a town and at this time people should be up and moving. However, the large police presence had told the townsfolk that something major was happening and everybody was staying low.

Finally they reached the end of the street and Louise hauled on the bar again to turn the vehicle so that it pointed right. Towards the sun. Morrell quickly glanced at the sky and saw that the sun wasn't quite in position yet and so beckoned her five helpers away.

'We've still got a little while until the sun is in position,' she said to them. They all nodded, although Sam could see that the two police officers didn't understand. However, they understood that Sam was running this operation and so just accepted her decisions. 'It only needs two of us to open those doors.'

'I'll do it,' said Louise immediately.

Sam looked to her partner and saw the determination in Brody's eyes. Sam nodded and then asked, 'Do you know how to open those doors?'

'Sure,' replied Brody. 'I was taught what to do at Quantico and I did pretty well in my class.'

'Fine. You open the lock and I'll haul the doors open,' Sam told her. 'As soon as the lock is disengaged you get your ass out of the way, understood?'

Louise nodded.

'That way we'll keep casualties to a minimum. I learnt

how dangerous these women are the last time I did this,' Sam finished.

'You've done this before?' asked the deputy.

'Yes, although nowhere near as carefully as we're doing it today,' Sam replied. 'As I've said, these women are extremely dangerous, so keep your heads down.'

Just before walking back to the police line, Jeffson stuck out his hand and said, 'Good luck, Sam; you too, Louise.'

'Thanks, Paul,' said Sam, shaking his hand. 'We owe them for Tacoma; today sees the end to this.' And she couldn't hide her relief at this prospect.

Louise took a lock-gun, a device used by law enforcement for opening locked doors without damaging them. Then she stood by Sam, halfway between the police line and the Dodge Caravan. There they waited for the sun to move into its optimum position.

They waited for about twenty minutes until the sun was shining straight down the street, and then Sam said, 'Okay, Louise, now's the time.'

'Sure thing.' Brody's voice shook slightly. Morrell reached out and gently squeezed Brody's hand.

The two women walked over to the Dodge's rear doors and Sam repeated to Louise, 'Once you've unlocked the doors, get the hell out.'

'What about you?' Louise asked.

'I'll be right in front of you.' Sam grinned.

Louise nodded and put the nozzle of the lock-gun to the lock on the rear doors. Sam took up position beside her and gently took hold of both of the door handles. Louise took a deep breath and then gently squeezed the trigger. There was a quiet grating sound as the gun connected with the door lock, then *Thock!*

The lock opened. Louise scrambled to her left and made for the police line and Sam hauled open both doors. An inhuman shrieking issued from the van as she reached in, grabbed a pair of ankles and hauled a body out of the rear before dashing for the police line herself.

Comfortable, cocooning darkness; unconsciousness. Then bright, white searing agony. Chloe immediately awoke, screaming with unbelievable pain; she could hardly see, it was so bright. Maggie and Jen were also awake and screaming. Chloe could see that their faces had blackened and charred, that smoke was *streaming* out of their seared flesh. She saw a dark figure pull Isa out of the van and Chloe watched in horror as Isa's entire face immediately blackened and shrivelled and smoked. Exposed to direct sunlight, Maggie and Jen reacted instinctively and both of them dived through the windshield, bouncing on the hood of the van before rolling off it out of sight. But Isa!

Chloe was in mortal agony, but Isa's screams cut through and Chloe, still holding her blanket, jumped out of the rear of the van and threw half of the blanket over Isa's head. She kept the other half to cover herself.

With the direct sunlight blocked out, Isa brought herself back and said to Chloe, 'We've got to find shade!'

Chloe thought for a moment and then said, 'Front of the van!'

The two women, agonised and weakened, staggered around to the front of the van where Maggie and Jen were cowering under another blanket.

'Jesus!' moaned Jen. 'Another minute of this and we're finished.'

'Hang on!' cried Maggie and then she screamed as she ducked out from under the blanket she and Jen were sharing and jumped onto the hood of the Dodge. Moaning in pain and with smoke pouring out of her blackened flesh, Maggie reached in through the broken windshield and hauled out their bags from the front seats.

Jen ripped open the holdall and began handing out the towels, gloves and goggles.

205

'This'll only buy us a couple more minutes,' said Isa. Her voice was teary. 'We have to get under cover and out of the sun!'

'I know,' replied Jen, surveying the area and not liking what she saw. The nearest heavy shade was over thirty yards away and had a cordon of heavily armed police in front of it. 'Whoever did this knew what they were doing. Shit!' And she frantically began patting out the flames that had sprung up on her arm.

'Oh Chloe,' said Maggie in a tearful voice, 'I'm so sorry.' Her gloved hand gently cupped the teenager's cheek.

'That's okay,' replied Chloe, who, despite having her bare flesh covered, was still smoking alarmingly. 'Joining you guys was the best thing that ever happened to me. I wouldn't have missed it for the world.' She snuggled closer to her partner and asked, 'If we're going down shall we take some of them with us?'

Jen thought for a moment and then answered, 'No, what's the use? They've got us right out in the open and have arranged it so that they can keep us here.' She indicated the armoured policemen armed with shotguns. 'As I said, someone knew what they were doing.' She looked to Isa and said, 'We had a good run though.'

'Yeah,' agreed Isa, her voice almost breaking. 'Coming up for five centuries now. Can't really complain.'

And with that all four of them huddled close together under the blankets in the meagre shade of the Dodge. There they waited for the end.

After pulling one of them out into the open, Sam had run like hell for the police line.

'What the fuck are you doing?' Louise practically screamed at her.

'Making sure of at least one of them,' Sam replied and

turned to see the woman she had pulled out screaming and smoking. Sam saw the reaction of the police officers to what was happening and realised that some of them might actually bolt and run. This was beyond their experience; most people didn't smoke like that in the sunlight.

'Hold your positions!' Sam said to them through a bullhorn. 'Just keep them in the sunlight!'

Sam then saw Chloe Lamont leap out of the back of the van and cover the other woman with a blanket. They then staggered to the front of the van to join the other two who had crashed through the windshield.

'Shit!' exclaimed Sam. 'I forgot that the vehicle would cast a shadow.'

'What do you mean?' asked Louise.

'Look where they're crouching.' Sam pointed. 'They're out of the direct sunlight.'

'Doesn't matter,' said Brody after a couple of moments. 'They're still smoking pretty good and they're starting to catch fire.' As she spoke, one of them patted out some flames on her arm.

Even after Maggie had pulled the bags out of the vehicle and the quartet had covered themselves they were still suffering the effects of being exposed to daylight. Above the group the air shimmered with expended heat.

'It's only a matter of time now,' said Sam in a regretful tone as she watched them all huddle together. The truth was she felt sorry for them; it must be agony to burn like they were, but it was the only way she knew of dealing with them.

'We've got them,' said Louise in a hushed voice. 'We've actually got them. We're gonna finish this!'

Famous last words.

From nearby came the screams of car engine and tyres followed by the crash of splintering wood. From behind the cordon, down the road to Morrell's left, a vehicle burst

207

forth from another storage building sending chunks of wood flying in all directions. Tyres squealed as the car bore right and then smashed through the cordon. The police had blocked the road with their cars in a classic 'V' shape with the point in the direction of the Dodge to prevent it from escaping. However, this meant that a vehicle coming from the other direction would find it very easy to smash through.

That vehicle was a cream-and-brown station wagon.

After punching through the cordon it jammed its brakes on and spun through one hundred and eighty degrees, coming to a halt some eight feet from the quartet. The passenger door opened and Maggie, Jen and Isa were stunned to see Chloe leaning across and screaming, 'GET IN!' at them.

'GO!' screamed the real Chloe, leaping to her feet and pulling her gun out. She emptied the clip at the police line, reloaded and emptied another clip; police officers dived for cover.

After a stunned moment the other three rose up, pulled their guns and directed suppressing fire at the surrounding police as they made to get in the vehicle. Chloe opened the wagon's rear hatch and jumped in, and Maggie went with her. Isa climbed in the rear door, Jen the front.

Even before the doors were all closed the station wagon pulled away with screaming, smoking rubber and drove straight through the gap it had created on entering the killing zone. The car made a screaming hard left into the warehouse from which it had emerged and punched out through its back wall to enter the near warren of service roads in this part of town.

Jen, sitting in the front, regarded the Chloe that was driving with wide eyes. She was dressed differently, lighter coloured jeans and a navy blue bomber jacket. She was unmarked by sunburn and had an earpiece in. Jen looked to the back of the car and saw Chloe was there too; she was blackened but had the hugest grin you'd ever seen on her face.

'Hiya Raych!' crowed Chloe.

Rachael, thought Jen. *Chloe's twin, of course!*

'Shush, I'm listening in to them!' said the other girl.

Jen then saw what the earpiece was for, this girl was listening in to the police radio to get a fix on where the authorities were stationed. Jen then suddenly realised that she wasn't burning in the car, Rachael had darkened it! There was tinfoil covering every window except for a strip of dark window tint at driver's eye level; how did this girl know what to do?

'Hang on tight, ladies,' said Rachael. 'The town's crawling with cops and state patrol and I've got to try and punch through the defensive lines they've put down.'

After that she said no more and concentrated on driving at breakneck speed through the narrow service roads.

'JESUS CHRIST!' screamed Morrell as she watched the station wagon roar away. 'STOP THAT FUCKING CAR!'

The police scurried in all directions; Duganis was on a police-car radio shouting instructions to the officers stationed in the town; patrol cars roared after the station wagon with their sirens wailing. Morrell just stood there with slumped shoulders and wide, disbelieving eyes. She'd had them! She'd had them!

And then she'd lost them.

But it wasn't over yet. There was still plenty of daylight left and whilst the sun was up these women were vulnerable. But now that they were awake the police had lost the initiative.

'Can we call in the National Guard?' Morrell asked Jeffson. 'Rip that car apart with a missile?'

'Are you serious?' demanded Jeffson.

'Paul, the only way to stop them is to trap them in the

sunlight!' Morrell was now frantic. 'Those girls are awake now and if anyone goes near that car then they're gonna get their heads blown off.'

'By the time we get the Guard arranged it'll be past nightfall,' Jeffson said.

'Shit!'

Morrell, Brody, Jeffson and Duganis went back to the MCV to co-ordinate the pursuit.

When nightfall came, despite an enormous pursuit, the station wagon was still at large.

Chapter 18

Jen didn't really have a chance to see where they were going as Isa was in floods of tears. Tears of pain but also of abject fear. Jen sympathised completely; she was scared out of her wits too. Being exposed to sunlight like that was the worst thing for them, so she wrapped her arms around Isa and they comforted one another.

After a short while Jen's head began to loll—she needed to sleep. She lowered the seatback until it was almost horizontal and made to lie down; Isa stretched across the rear seat so that she could lie close to Jen. Chloe and Maggie were already asleep in the very rear.

'Is there anything I should do if I need to wake you?' asked Rachael.

'Just scream "daylight" very loudly,' Jen replied drowsily. 'That'll get our attention.'

'Sure thing,' replied Rachael. 'Sweet dreams and I'll see you at sundown. Hopefully.'

Jen had laid her head down and fallen asleep with deep foreboding, believing that Rachael's intervention had only bought them a little more time. She expected to be woken up again that day by searing sunlight. She was therefore very surprised, not to mention relieved, when her eyes naturally opened as the sun dipped below the horizon. She raised her head slightly and she saw Isa's eyes open, saw in her partner's face what must have been written on hers:

wonderment at still being alive. She looked across to the driver's seat and saw that Rachael was fast asleep; to Jen she looked incredibly beautiful then. She reached out and gently shook their saviour, who woke up with a quiet snort and bleary eyes.

'Must be nightfall,' was her waking comment.

'It is,' said Jen. 'Thank you for saving us.'

'Chloe's my twin,' said Rachael, waving her hand dismissively. 'I don't think there's anything I wouldn't do for her. You other three benefited because you were with her.'

'Well, we're extremely grateful anyway,' said Jen. 'How did you know to darken the vehicle for us?'

'Because,' said Rachael, regarding Jen with serious eyes, 'for the last ten years you have been hunted.' And Rachael told them all about Sam Morrell's decade-long pursuit, using the printouts to show them just how exposed they had become.

When she finished there was a hushed silence in the car. It was finally broken by Isa.

'My word, your worst fear was realised, Jen.'

'I know,' replied Jen. 'And the only thing that really saved us these last six years was Morrell's inability to get the rest of the FBI after us.'

'And Morrell's still out there,' said Maggie. 'She'll never rest until she's killed us.'

'There's always Mexico,' Isa pointed out.

'Yeah, but she can alert the authorities down there about us. As wanted killers at the very least,' replied Maggie.

'We're just going to have to do something about her before we leave,' said Jen. There was murmured agreement. She then turned to Rachael and asked, 'How can we thank you?'

'Take me with you,' the girl replied.

'Do you realise what that entails?' Jen asked and Rachael nodded, her eyes nervous but her expression resolute.

'Rachael, once turned there's no turning back. Are you absolutely sure?'

Rachael smiled gently and said, 'Chloe's with you, that's where I want to be.'

Jen nodded.

'Are *you* sure, Jen?' asked Maggie in a worried voice. 'That'll make five of us, we'll be that little bit easier to detect.'

'We have no choice,' Jen told Maggie. 'We owe Rachael our lives. If she wants to come over then that's what we'll do for her. It's all we've really got to offer.'

Maggie smiled and nodded.

Jen looked to Isa, who smiled and then leant over the driver's seat and gently bit Rachael's neck.

'Welcome, sister,' she whispered into the girl's ear.

Night had fallen and Sam was devastated; despite a huge police search, no trace of the station wagon had been found. It was as though it had vanished into thin air. Louise was with her, arm around her shoulders, comforting her.

'Don't worry, Sam. We'll figure something out.'

Sam didn't reply, she just stood there with her head on Louise's shoulder, wondering why her? She heard footsteps approaching and so raised her head and turned around. Walking towards her were Jeffson, Duganis and Sheriff Baylock; all three had grim expressions. Sam didn't need them to say that they still hadn't traced the fugitives.

'I need a beer,' she said to them.

'We all do,' replied Duganis. 'You did real good today, Sam, no one else could have done better.' He looked as devastated as she felt.

'Yeah, but I got outsmarted by a kid from a backyard, New Mexico shithole,' she said, utterly depressed.

'We all did,' said Jeffson quietly. 'I'd like to catch her

213

and find out how she did it. There's an important lesson to be learned there.'

'You don't want to go anywhere near Rachael Lamont now,' Sam said. 'They'll turn her as a thank-you. My God, there's five of them now!'

'Come on,' said Duganis. 'Let's get that beer. Sheriff? I do believe you've earned one.'

Baylock smiled gently, nodded and said, 'I know a nice quiet bar, follow me.' And he led them down a quiet side street.

As they were walking, Sam noticed that the road was very dark and she realised that several streetlamps were out of action. As they entered the dark area Sam saw a car parked on the other side of the road. As she got closer she was able to make out its shape.

A station wagon.

'I don't believe it!' she said in a quiet, teary voice. She crossed the road to the car.

'What?' asked Louise and then she saw it. 'Jesus, they never left town!'

The other three had seen the car and crossed the road. Duganis said, 'Do you know what this means?'

'Yes,' replied Sam, tears streaming down her face. 'It means we're all dead.'

'What?' replied Louise. 'Oh . . .' But she never finished what she was about to say as there was a blur of movement in the shadows and Morrell's four companions were set upon by the quartet.

Sam could have run for it but what was the use? They'd kill her before she had taken three steps, so she sat on the hood of the wagon and watched in horrid fascination as these predators she had been pursuing for so long fed in front of her. After feeding, the one closest to her dropped the corpse of Louise Brody, wiped the blood from her mouth and looked Morrell straight in the eye.

214

'Maggie O'Hearn,' said Sam in a neutral tone.

'None other; Samantha Morrell,' replied Maggie.

'You know me and I know you,' said Sam. 'I also know Chloe and Rachael here.' She indicated the twins. 'I even found Caitlin Baker but . . .' She looked over at the other two women and said, 'I was never able to find you two.'

'Geneviève Albiére,' said Jen.

'Isabella Contracelli,' said Isa.

'Europeans,' said Morrell, nodding. 'I thought as much. You came over here during the War for Independence?'

Both women nodded and Jen said, 'You're a formidable woman, Sam, you spent ten years chasing us and in that time you learned a lot about us. We, on the other hand, had no idea you even existed. That makes you very dangerous.'

'Not tonight though,' Sam pointed out. 'This is your time and I'm powerless against you.' She turned to Rachael. 'You took a huge risk by staying in the town. Where did you hide out?'

'Under a tarpaulin behind the storage shed they were originally parked in,' replied Rachael. 'Out of sight is out of mind. I figured that would be the last place you'd look.'

'Jesus!' muttered Morrell, putting her head in her hands.

Maggie had been regarding Sam with mounting anger during the exchange. Now that anger emerged icily. 'You killed Caitlin.' Her tone was *very* unfriendly. 'I ought to rip your face off for that.'

'What else was I supposed to do?' Sam countered, looking up.

'You could leave us in peace!' said Maggie belligerently.

Sam gave a quiet, humourless laugh, reached into her jacket and pulled out her ID. She showed it to Maggie. 'You kill people,' she stated. 'It's my job to stop that.'

After a few moments' consideration Maggie nodded and said, 'I can accept that but it still doesn't ease the pain for me. I was with Caitlin for a long time.'

215

'I know,' replied Sam, her voice gentle, wondering. 'Nearly a century. However, you survived that incident, and this one. You're a lucky girl, I'm not.' And she put her head back in her hands. 'Christ! I'm so tired,' she said quietly.

'Well, you can rest now, Samantha,' whispered Jen, her face close to Sam's.

'Thank God,' said Sam as the quartet surrounded her.

Epilogue

'It's an absolute pleasure feeding you,' Isa said, smiling down at Rachael. Just like her sister, Rachael instinctively knew when she was bringing the one feeding her down to the danger level, so she voluntarily raised her head.

'It's no surprise really, is it?' Maggie said to Isa. 'They are twins, after all.'

Rachael wiped her mouth and stood up, her eyes bright. Chloe slung an arm around her sibling's shoulders and the two of them put their cheeks together and grinned at the women, grins that promised much mischief.

'Watch out, world,' said Isa, rolling her eyes but with a warm smile. 'There's two of 'em!'

Chloe laughed and asked, 'We ready to move yet?'

'We will be once Jen's finished,' replied Maggie. They all looked over to where Jen was.

'That's enough!' said Jen sternly, yanking her arm up and away. Then her face softened and she said, 'If I let you drink your fill you can easily drain me and I'd probably die.' She then smiled and asked, 'How do you feel?'

'Magnificent,' replied Morrell with a soft smile and wondering eyes as she wiped the blood from her lips and chin. Then her expression turned pained and she asked, 'Why didn't you just kill me?'

'Because,' began Jen, squatting down so that she was eye level with Sam, 'we need you. You nearly caught us twice which means we have to alter our habits. One immovable law of nature is adapt or die; we need to adapt if we're to survive. You were a police officer so you know how they investigate, you can teach us how to feed in order to avoid detection. Also, there's your case file on us—that needs to be destroyed.'

'There's stuff about you in police departments all over the country,' Sam pointed out. 'You won't be able to erase all those.'

'I know,' replied Jen. 'But your main file along with twenty or so years south of the border should be enough to see us safe. People do have short memories.'

'Some do,' agreed Sam. 'And some don't,' she added, remembering Mort Larney from Brody's hometown.

'Come on, Sam,' said Jen, standing up and offering a hand to her newest sister. 'Let's get moving, a couple more days in the States and then off to Central America for a while.'

'Okay,' said Sam with a smile; the truth was she loved being what Jen and the others were already. Right at what she thought was the end, that darkened street in Carthage, she had no fight left in her whatsoever. The prospect of being killed that night was a welcome one for Sam, relief at not having to go on any more. But she hadn't been killed; instead she had been *turned* and that had given her a brand-new lease of life. She felt so alive, so vital that she almost felt seventeen again! She took Jen's hand and stood up, and then she kissed the other woman on the cheek. 'Thank you.' Her voice was husky, choked by so much gratitude.

'*De nada,*' said Jen with a smile. She regarded Sam a moment; her eyes were filled with simple fondness and affection. Then she leaned in and kissed Sam full on the mouth. 'We are a family, Sam,' she told the former FBI agent. 'And you are now a part of it.'

They walked over to where the others were and Isa,

Maggie, Chloe and Rachael all had warm hugs for Sam. Afterwards her eyes glistened with tears.

They all climbed into a brand-new Winnebago, expertly stolen by Isa, and headed off into the night. Their destination was Washington, DC, the Hoover Building in particular. As they travelled, Sam reflected on the hand fate had dealt her; after ten years of pursuit, death was a poor reward for that kind of dedication really. This new life though, well, what could she say? She was happy, loved and *alive*; what more could she wish for?

Nothing. She had everything now. Well, nearly everything. All that was left was for her to find a partner to share the endless centuries ahead with. That would come in due time and Sam wasn't fretting about it; for now, it was more than enough to live in the night with her sisters.

Sam's case file was deleted from the Bureau's computer system, as was the back-up copy. The hard copy of the case also went missing out of Sam's office, shredded. The FBI did investigate the murders of three of its agents in Carthage and the disappearance of Morrell, but with no case file to go on and no clues they discovered nothing despite APB's on Sam, Chloe and Rachael. The last record of them was on the Hoover Building's CCTV when they entered during the small hours. They simply disappeared after that last sighting, with no one the wiser about the existence of Maggie, Jen and Isa. But they were out there . . .

. . . and always would be.